THE SCARLET CORD

Hannah MacFarlane

First published 2009
ISBN 978 1 84427 370 6

Scripture Union
207-209 Queensway, Bletchley, Milton Keynes, MK2 2EB
Email: info@scriptureunion.org.uk
Website: www.scriptureunion.org.uk

Scripture Union Australia
Locked Bag 2, Central Coast Business Centre, NSW 2252
Website: www.scriptureunion.org.au

Scripture Union USA
PO Box 987, Valley Forge, PA 19482
Website: www.scriptureunion.org

British Library Cataloguing-in-Publication Data
A catalogue record of this book is available from the British Library.

Printed and bound in India by Thomson Press India Ltd

Cover design: GoBallistic
Illustrations: Helen Jones

For Adiella

Names used

	Name	*Meaning*	*Origin*
	Sekani	Laughs	Egyptian
	Tabia	Talented	Egyptian
	Daya	Bird	Hebrew
	Gurion	Lion cub	Hebrew

PART ONE: JERICHO

"All the peoples of the earth will see that you [Israel] are called by the name of the Lord, and they will be afraid of you."

1

"Go; view the land, especially Jericho."

"Move it, Tabia! Run!"

I'm telling you, the rats in this shabby street move faster than my sister. Anyone would think she was out for an afternoon stroll on the city wall...

"Get behind here! Quick!"

She's caught up - finally - and squats down, puffing and panting like an overloaded donkey. I pull her back against the wall and chance a quick glance over the soaked and smelly bundles of barley heaped up all higgledy-piggledy in front of us. It's more than my life's worth to be seen anywhere near here right now, but I can't miss this - not for anything! The adrenaline is still pumping round my body from running flat out just now and the thrill of having got away with this makes that buzzing feeling I have even better; it's a feeling of power. Like I imagine it would feel to be king. Yes, there is - technically - already one king in Jericho. But he isn't ever likely to come and visit this part of town. He'll stay within the inner wall where life is orderly and neat, where people behave as they should and everything runs on a tight schedule. Here though, it's different; here - in the scum, the muck and the grime - I feel like I'm king.

I live in the no-man's-land between the lofty inner wall that marks the city proper and the great outer barrier wall that keeps the wild world firmly shut out - affectionately known to most as "the slums". To me though, it's just home - a place of friends, fun and freedom. My parents don't always see things that way, but I'm pretty good at keeping a low profile where they're concerned.

This afternoon, for example, I'm supposed to be collecting the sun-dried flax from the roof of our house and combing out the seeds. Really, I'm watching a performance by some of our top local street entertainers - also known as my neighbours. I've engineered the whole thing to perfection, like a royal puppeteer, and the fun is just beginning...

"What's happening, Sekani? What can you see?" whispers an anxious voice next to me. My sister has stopped gasping for breath and wants to know what's happening on the other side of the great barley bundles.

"It's great! That short woman who never talks to anyone has just stumbled out of her front door, still in her nightwear. She's trying to figure out who knocked, but she's a bit dazed by the daylight. Looks like we woke her up!"

"What about the grumpy one? Where's she?"

"Out on the street too. The baby's screaming again, the boys are clinging onto her legs, and she's trying to pick her clothes out of the dirt. She seems really annoyed! Oh, this is brilliant! Look!"

But she doesn't. My sister's funny like that. She's enjoying her part in creating this chaos just as much as I am - she practically masterminded the whole thing - and yet she can't bear to actually see the scene for herself. She gets me to tell her, so she can imagine it all happening in her head. Me? I live for the action, first hand. It's why we work together so well, I suppose.

"What? What are they doing?"

"Come and look! They won't see you, they're too busy..."

"No. I can't," she whispers. "Just tell me what's happening. Please, Sekani."

"All right. The silent one grabbed the nearest child to stop her making so much noise! Old grump's in a proper rage about that. She's just yanked her daughter away and is ranting in the middle of the street. The two old sisters who usually sit on their front step are both on their feet to get a better view and everyone's coming out of their houses to see what all the fuss is! Hang on - soldiers!"

High on the wall above us, two of the king's men are making their regular patrol. It's part of their official duty, but they're not just doing it because they have to. The soldiers love to use their status and their commanding position on the inner wall to remind those of us who live in the slums just how small, worthless and insignificant we really are. I pull Tabia further back against the wall.

"Oi!" yells one of the soldiers to the bickering women. "Stop that noise!" The women crane their necks to look up at the men on the wall.

"You're yapping like dogs in the streets," adds the other, "I suppose we can't expect much more from your kind." He spits in their direction and the globule lands heavily on the ground between them. The soldiers turn away to continue their patrol and the women resume their row as if nothing had happened.

I peer out over the barley again. "Now the men are coming back, Tabia... Oh, the timing couldn't be better! They're back from the fields with the barley and the street is totally blocked by all the women. The men are ordering the women aside, forcing their way through, dripping gunk all over the washing..."

"They're back with more barley?"

"Yes, and they're—"

"They're going to want to stack it here with the rest. Come on, we have to move!"

She's right! I'm so carried away in the mayhem we created that I hadn't thought about that. The men are going to stack the sodden barley harvest right where we're hiding, and if we're seen hiding here, they'll know straight away that we're up to something. We're not exactly strangers to trouble; everyone here knows not to trust us - mostly from personal experience. I scramble to my feet and tear along the street after Tabia, keeping close in to the wall until we've put enough distance between us and our crime.

"Well done, Tabia. Best plan so far this week and you got us out just in time!"

"Thanks. Shame we missed the end though."

"Yes... But you should have seen the bickering! It was a stroke of genius to get them blaming each other. Brilliant! What shall we do now?"

"Well..." She sounds unusually hesitant. "We're supposed to have the roof cleared before dinner—"

Why does she have to remind me of that, just when life was feeling so good? How can someone so devious also be so dull? I'm attempting to revel in the glory of the moment and my sister is talking about chores.

"—and that doesn't give us very long. Perhaps we should get back."

I kick the wall in frustration and drag my feet deliberately, desperately trying to think of an alternative that will persuade Tabia not to go home just yet. I'm not the one with all the ideas though, she is. If only I could...

I'm so wrapped up in feeling sorry for myself that I almost don't notice the two unfamiliar men overtaking us. Almost. But there's something obviously strange about them that distracts me, even from my total annoyance at having a perfectly good afternoon spoiled so soon. They're not from my territory. And I'm fairly sure they're not city dwellers either. Who would be coming to Jericho? And why wouldn't they go straight through the slums, heads down, avoiding eye contact until they reach "true" civilisation? Everyone else does. They must *want* to avoid presenting themselves to the king. That's odd. I pick up my pace to follow them. Tabia has spotted them too; she does the same, being careful not to be noticed. We're good at blending in though. It's an important skill to have when you make a habit of disturbing the peace for your own amusement.

2

"Bring out the men who have entered your house."

Sekani has just picked up his pace. That means he's finally caught on to what's happening beyond the end of his own nose! I wish he'd make it a little less obvious though. He keeps giving me these really unsubtle sideways looks and jerking his head towards the two men. It's a good thing they're so busy trying to keep a low profile themselves, or they'd almost certainly have noticed my brother's odd behaviour.

I'd already spotted the two men when the barley harvesters arrived back. They were just passing our hiding spot and obviously had the same concern about being seen there as Sekani and I. They started to stride more purposefully and quickly attracted my interest. Who are they? What are they doing here in the slums? The presence of two strangers can only mean one thing: adventure. Somebody's up to something even more suspicious than we are! I had to know more. The only problem was that to escape being caught at the scene of our own crime we had no choice but to sprint ahead of them. I then had to think of a way to slow right down again and get the men back in our sights. And what was the obvious solution? To make Sekani think we were heading for home; there's nothing he hates more!

My little brother is totally predictable like that. He's the outdoor type. He hates being restricted; by walls, by time, by our parents… It doesn't matter what it is. If it threatens his sense of independence, then it must be bad! I probably know Sekani better than anyone else and I'd say that his worst nightmare is being a part of something. As far as he's concerned, he's something all by himself. I'm using this to my advantage just now. Anyway, it amuses me to see what I can guide him into, without him realising I'm doing it. It makes me feel secretly powerful.

Look! This gets more fascinating by the minute! I hadn't predicted this twist at all. We've been moving gradually northwards, finding ourselves closer to home than is really comfortable. I've even been working on a strategy to keep on their trail without my parents seeing us and dragging us back inside the house, but it didn't occur to me for a second that the mischief-makers would lead us right to our own front door! My aunt is listening to them at the door. She'll soon send them on their way… No – she's inviting them in! What can they possibly be doing here? Fantastic – we'd usually have to go in search of action, but here is a ready-made adventure awaiting us in our own home. There is one big dilemma though. How do we get in on the action, without being turned out on our ears? I know that the moment we enter the house we'll be disciplined for the uncombed flax. But if we don't go in, we'll be missing out on the biggest intrigue this family has ever seen.

"So?" demands Sekani, a look of impatient expectation painted across his round face.

"So...?" I play for time, watching him enjoy explaining the details to me as if I had no idea of the problem. I only half-listen to his words though, weighing up instead the choice between trying to sneak in unnoticed in the excitement of the strangers' arrival versus picking up as much as we can from listening at the window and then catching up with the men again on their way out. Neither option is as sound as I'd like.

"Tabia, are you listening to me?"

"Mmm? What?"

"They're in there and we're out here, not finding out a single thing about who they are or what they're doing here! So what's our plan of action?"

"Well..." I begin slowly, still thinking on my feet, but something I notice over Sekani's shoulder makes my mind up faster than the flow of the Jordan in flood. He looks keenly at me, frustrated not so much by my unfinished sentence as by the time being wasted while he's not actually doing anything. He's kicking up the dust with his toes.

"Tabia?"

I whirl him around and point at the people disappearing rapidly into their homes. The streets are all but deserted in a matter of moments. We watch together as at the far end of the street a handful of the king's men make their way along the street towards us, stopping only to ask directions from the silent woman we played our trick on earlier. The woman stares stubbornly at them, hand outstretched, until a valuable scarab is pressed bitterly into her grubby palm.

"What are they doing here?" breathes Sekani. But we both already know the answer. The coincidence is too great. The scene is as predictable as the hot sun in the day: the bribed hand rises to point towards the doorway where we are standing; the king's men turn to face us. Whatever telling off awaits us inside the house is less dangerous by far than these men. Sekani is already shoving his way through the door and I follow hastily to warn the others.

Before I've even closed the door… "Where have you two been all this time?" The predictable question hits me.

"Mum, the king has sent men. They're out—"

"Tabia! This is not the time for wild adventure stories. I asked you where you were today." *How much time is there? How can I explain?*

"It's true. They're out there now and they're coming to the house. They're already on the way." I can tell she doesn't believe me and is already growing angry. Her eyes have narrowed. I struggle to think of a way to convince her quickly, but I can't. Panic is rising inside my chest. Instead, I blurt out the only thought in my head: "Soldiers!" Catapulting into action at the sound of this word, my aunt springs up and breaks off her conversation with the men. She looks from me to Sekani and back again. I think she knows something. She seems serious, but purposeful. She certainly seems to know I'm telling the truth.

“Tabia. Sekani. I need you to hide these two men. They must not be found here. It is very important. Can I trust you?” We nod our agreement in chorus. “Go quickly!”

I grab Sekani’s arm and gesture for the men to follow as I scramble out of the room.

“Where are we go—?” Sekani begins. I reply without hesitation.

“The roof!”

3

"I do not know where they went."

Tabia is glaring at me. It takes me a moment or two to realise why. My leg is twitching rapidly up and down, which annoys her. It does this by itself - I can't help it - especially at times like this, when I'm forced to sit still. I need to move. It's unnatural just to sit here like this, waiting. I pick up the comb that has dropped from my hand and insert its teeth between the strands of flax on my lap. I don't actually comb them though. I'm trying really hard to listen and the sound of dried seeds falling on the ground would not exactly be helpful. Tabia is still staring. With great effort, I shift my weight and stop my leg from jiggling. I don't know why it bothers her so much.

How can she sit there so calmly anyway? As we wait here, the king's men are talking with my aunt. The king's men! Soldiers who would love any excuse to inflict punishment on us simple slum-dwellers - or worse, imprison us! And the men they're here to search for are lying inches away from me, buried under a large mound of dried flax. If they are found here, and Tabia and I are found guarding them... I can't even think about it. My leg is already twitching again and I'm literally biting my tongue to stop myself blurting out the questions that are buzzing around in my head.

I feel angry with these two total strangers. How can they come here and endanger us like this? Don't they realise what it could mean for us? And we don't even know what they want. I'm beginning to feel sick with dread, thinking of all the worst scenarios. If only I knew what was going on down there... I slowly push myself up, being careful not to make a sound as I lay down the stalks on the ground. I look across at Tabia. She is shaking her head, her eyes fixed on me in warning. She's probably right, but the fear is taking over. I tear my eyes away and head deliberately towards the steps. She knows better than to try to stop me.

I can hear the low rumble of voices below as I creep down the stairs. I don't want to miss a word, but I'm having to move extremely slowly. I can't risk drawing attention to myself, and possibly also to Tabia and the outsiders on the roof. I get as close as I dare, and then lower myself onto a step and lean forward, forcing all thoughts from my mind so I can listen properly.

"Two Israelite men were seen entering this house," insists one of the king's men. I get the impression it is not the first time he has said this. There's a definite tone of impatience in his voice.

The next voice I hear belongs to my aunt. It is as calm and untroubled as the sacred lake water in the legendary temples of Egypt.

"Yes. They were here."

What? Is she mad? They'll search the entire place and they're bound to find the men! What is she thinking? I'm torn between staying where I am and sprinting back to warn Tabia. Maybe if we're not actually found with the men, we'll be spared. We can say that we didn't know they were here. Yes. That's what we'll do. I'll go to tell Tabia now.

But I find that I can't actually move. I sit rooted to my step and listen harder still as a third voice joins the conversation.

"Bring out the men. They have come to search the land."

This is not looking good. I very carefully push myself up onto my feet and turn away from the scene. I must get to Tabia before the soldiers come.

"I didn't know where they were from." It's my aunt. I dither on the step. She's lying. She was talking with the men; she must have known. I know that she's trying to protect the family, but there seems to be more to it than that. Is she protecting these strangers too? Why? It could make everything so much worse for us all. There's silence below. I imagine the king's men are trying to decide whether or not to believe her. My aunt carries on.

"When it was time to shut the gate at dark, the men went out. Chase them quickly and you'll catch them." I hold my breath. I'm quite used to hiding out and waiting for trouble to pass, but this is different somehow. It's unbearable. This is not just the threat of a beating for causing chaos on the streets. This is real danger, and it involves my whole family. My heart is pounding and I realise that I'm actually scared. This is not the same adrenaline rush I enjoy when Tabia dreams up a good plan; it's not the nervous excitement of watching from a distance as my trick is discovered. My palms are sweaty and my mind is racing. I don't like it at all. Finally, a door bangs shut and I hear footsteps hurrying away down the street. Relief floods over me, allowing my body to relax and I burst clumsily into the downstairs room.

"Sekani, where are they? I must speak with them quickly."

"On the roof. We hid them under the—" But my aunt is already sweeping past me. I'm right behind her. This is my chance to make sense of what's happening here and I'm not going to miss it. I arrive on the roof in time to see the men scrambling out from under the flax and brushing themselves off. I open my mouth to speak but I get a meaningful look from my aunt: the one that says, "You need to go now, Sekani. I don't want you to hear this." My eyes widen in disbelief and fury. After we just risked our lives to hide these men for her, she's not even going to give us an explanation! Adults are so unfair! I look to Tabia for support. "We need to hear this," I try to tell her without speaking. But, bizarrely, she's accepted the hint and is making her way towards the steps. Even my big sister is not backing me up!

"Tabia, surely you—" but she grabs my hand and leads me away before I can finish the sentence. I'm about to give her a real mouthful - I can't believe that she didn't support my protest - and my anger is stirring. It's not going to be kept in much longer. As soon as we get downstairs I'm going to let her know exactly what I think!

But we don't get downstairs. In fact, we don't get very far at all before my rage is replaced by a new sense of deep admiration for my sister. She takes us just far enough that my aunt thinks we've gone, five or six steps at most, and pulls me down to a crouching position to listen. I grin. It's obvious really. If she'd let me protest, we'd have been bundled downstairs by our aunt and lectured by our mother. Then we'd have missed everything. My sister is a genius! How does she think of these brilliant plans in the heat of the moment? I must remember to thank her.

"I know the Lord has given you the land," my aunt is saying to the men. I shake my head in bewilderment. *The Lord? Land? What's she talking about?* "We heard what you did beyond the Jordan..." I miss the next few words because my mind has gone into overdrive, but I'm soon brought back to my senses by the shocking words "... utterly destroyed."

"Utterly destroyed?" I hiss at Tabia. "Utterly destroyed? Who are these men, Tabia, and what do they want with us?" I'm beginning to think we should have turned them in to the king's men after all. They seem outright dangerous.

"Shhh." She's listening intently.

"Swear to me by the Lord..." The Lord again. I'm confused. This is not getting any clearer. "... since I have dealt kindly with you..." *Kindly? Now that's an understatement. We saved their lives!* "... that you also will deal kindly with my father's household." Oh, I get it - she's bargaining with them! That is a really clever move, especially if these men really are as dangerous as they seem. *We saved your lives... I suddenly feel proud of my aunt... you save ours.* "Give me a pledge of truth and spare my father and my mother and my brothers and my sisters, with all who belong to them, and deliver our lives from death." Yes! I hold my breath for the answer.

"Our life for yours if you do not tell this business of ours."

I jump up. I need to go somewhere we can talk. There's so much to figure out and I can't contain my excitement. My own aunt has made a pact with genuinely treacherous men while Jericho's soldiers are out there looking for them. And yet they're willing to protect us. This is real adventure and I plan to be at the very centre of it!

4

"No courage remained in any man."

"The Israelites are coming here?"

The crowded room fell unusually quiet as a mass of stunned faces looked up one by one from their beakers of spiced beer to locate the source of such an outrageous statement. There was an uncomfortable pause as people who'd been pouring drinks sloppily from jars replaced the stoneware onto the low tables with resounding thuds and others shuffled to get comfortable, or jostled each other to get a better view. Eventually, the last sounds died away as a sense of expectation spread through the room. All eyes were focused intently on a solid-built man who everyone seemed to sense had posed the question, and on Rahab, from whom it seemed the man expected an answer. At the back of the room, two children crouched behind a low table, listening with more interest than anyone else present.

"Yes. The Israelites are coming here."

A wave of whispers swept the room. Some people held their breath, others let out gasps and moans; one man coughed and spluttered, trying unsuccessfully to swallow a large mouthful of beer which now dribbled unpleasantly from the corners of his mouth. The noise level rose quickly with wild gossip and anxious enquiries. The atmosphere came alive with concern. Then, above the din, a slurred voice from the back of the crowd boomed out.

"That's a good one, Rahab. Israelites! Ha! I nearly believed you. What a joke!"

After a slight pause of confusion, the room erupted with wild laughter as people revelled in what they were all too relieved to think had been Rahab's idea of humour. They took up their beakers again, slapped each other heartily and relaxed into smiles.

"I wasn't joking," said Rahab's small calm voice, and though it was barely a whisper in the rowdy room, her words were surprisingly audible. "Their spies were here today. The nation of Israel is approaching Jericho with its army, and they intend to conquer our land."

"You're serious? Rahab?"

"She is. She's serious!" The responses came thick and fast.

"Israel? But did you hear what they did to Sihon and Og?"

"Totally overcome!"

"Nothing left of them!"

"And you're sure they're coming here?"

"When? I mean, how long do we have?"

"What does it matter? There's nothing we can do. Didn't you hear how their God brought them out of Egypt? They escaped the Egyptians! Don't you see? We don't stand a chance."

"They crossed the Red Sea! Every last one of them! Amazing."

"Israel. I don't know what to say. Anyone else and we'd be all right… but Israel!"

"So, what are we going to do?"

"What can we do?"

"Nothing. It's hopeless."

"Well, I'm not going to sit around here and wait for them to arrive. I'm packing up my family and we're leaving first thing in the morning." The speaker got up from her table.

"Where will you go?"

"It doesn't matter. Anywhere but here."

"That's not a bad idea! We should all leave and save ourselves." Others now scrambled to their feet. In the chaos a jug smashed and thick brown liquid oozed down a table leg onto the floor. Nobody stopped to clean it up.

"They've shut the gate." This new, hoarse voice came from the shadows near the door. For the second time that evening, silence fell across the usually cheerful room. "I saw them, on my way here. Some of the king's men went out towards the fords, and the gate was barricaded behind them."

"But they'll open it again during the day, surely?"

"I don't know," croaked the voice. "The king knows that spies were here, and he will have guessed that Israel is not far behind. He won't be taking any chances."

"Then there's no way out?" The question was left hanging in the room. No one spoke or moved. The citizens of Jericho's slums had run out of things to say. Left with their thoughts and their beer, the sense of defeat hovered in the room like dust in the air.

Unnoticed by anyone, Sekani and Tabia crept discreetly away to reflect on what they'd heard. Their mother was still in the room, stunned and confused by the news. Her mind was reeling. She pulled Rahab to one side, away from the guests, and nervously stammered the only thought left in her head. She was already beginning to panic.

"Wh… what are we g… going—?"

"To do?" Rahab finished for her. Then she cautiously turned her back on the crowded room, put her head close to her sister's and spoke in the softest whisper. "Get the family together. I've arranged for us all to get out. The men are coming back for us because I helped them escape, but we can't tell anyone here… Wait 'til the neighbours have left… then explain to the others – and make sure that Tabia and Sekani know how important this is…"

Rahab paused to make sure her message was understood. "We must all wait inside the house until the men come for us."

5

"By a rope through her window."

"Sekani, did you hear that?"

"Tabia, I was right next to you. Of course I heard that!"

"Yes, all right, I know. But what they said was really significant. I just want to make sure you realise what it means." I'm standing in a narrow hallway face to face with my little brother, wishing that he didn't always insist on being so difficult. We're upstairs, out of earshot of the adults, but I don't know for how long. "It's not a game now, Sekani. This is serious."

"I know. It's brilliant, isn't it?"

I watch shadows flicker across my brother's face and try to decide whether or not he can see anything beyond his own excitement. Half of me thinks he grasps it all and is just toying with me, the other half thinks that maybe he's just too gripped by the drama to notice the threat. The dim light makes his straight-faced features even harder to read than usual: there's no twinkle in his eye, not even a slight curling of his lip to show that he might be teasing me. I decide to play it safe and spell out what I'm thinking.

"No, Sekani. It's not brilliant at all. It's dangerous."

"It's awesome! The whole of Jericho is scared senseless of Israel, there's going to be a battle – an actual battle – and we're on the winning side! Those Israelite spies have sworn to protect us."

"Are we talking about those same Israelite spies that you were really mad with not so long ago for leading soldiers to our house?"

"Yes, well. I overreacted."

"You overreacted?"

"All right, they may have put us in a tricky situation for a while. But we got out of it alive, didn't we? And they're promising to do more for our family than Jericho's soldiers have ever done. Plus…" Sekani pauses here for dramatic effect, a cheeky smile plastered on his face. "Plus, Tabia, this God of theirs seems to be worth finding out about, wouldn't you say? He's made some pretty weird stuff happen by all accounts, but always – every single time, Tabia – always to Israel's advantage. What has Jericho got going for it? A wall."

"A very large and important wall, Sekani. A wall that's protected you all your life."

"But it's still just a wall nonetheless: a wall that definitely can't make strange things happen; a wall behind which our soldiers plan to hide like cowards, rather than standing up and fighting like men. My bet is with those spies and their God. Listen, Tabia. Here's my plan: I'm going to—"

"Sekani, this is really not the kind of adventure we should—"

"It's exactly the kind of adventure we should get involved in, Tabia, because there's nothing to lose!"

"That's craziness, Sekani. Think about what you're saying!"

"I am thinking! Jericho is not going to survive this. You heard them say that even the king's men are worried."

"Yes, that's what I'm trying to… Israel will destroy us. You heard what they've done in the past to—"

"I know. They're awesome."

"…the Egyptians. And on the other side of the River Jordan. They're dangerous."

"Yes. Israel is very dangerous if you're an enemy. But that's because they're powerful. And if you're on their side – like we are now – power is a good thing. They've already sworn to protect us. And anyway, we won't be in Jericho when they come. We have to leave this city before we're destroyed with it. We'll go to where the men are, where the adventure is – to Israel." He looks at me for a moment, then adds, "Where they can make sure we're kept safe during the battle. And we'll be part of history and protected by the most powerful nation in the world!"

"Shhh!" I grab Sekani and drag him further along the dark hallway. "If anyone hears you talking like that we'll be reported. We're already in danger from these strange new travellers; we really don't want to upset our own authorities too." It's worse than I thought. Sekani is so blinded by the stories of Israel's greatness that he's determined to be involved at any cost. We don't even know whether we can trust these men. After all, why would they want to protect us? They were here for information. Now they've got it, they've deserted us. "It's too dangerous..."

Sekani draws himself up to look me straight in the eyes and says, "While we're out there, we can find the spies and make sure they keep their promise. We'll make sure the family get out, Tabia. All of them. It'll be our secret mission." He already has a plan. My uncertainty must show, because Sekani looks offended. "Do you have a better suggestion, Tabia?" He turns away, disappears through a nearby door and closes it behind him, leaving me to think.

He's insane! We can't just go and single-handedly rescue our entire family from a nation's attack. For a start, we can't get out of Jericho because the gate is barricaded and heavily guarded by soldiers. And even if we could, the rest of the family would be in enormous danger until we got back. Does he really think we can get those men to keep their promise of protecting one little household when they attack and destroy the entire city? I don't see how we could possibly persuade them. I have to talk to my brother.

I follow him through the door and Sekani immediately begins speaking again. I don't have a chance to reason with him. "Rahab trusts those men, Tabia. And I trust her judgement."

"Those men are not even here any more, Sekani. You heard Rahab explain that they 'were here today' – were! Where are they now? How are they going to protect us if they're not even—"

"They swore, Tabia. That's binding." I'm not convinced and Sekani knows it. "They can't go back on it now. They'll be here. They will."

"Look." He gestures me over to the window where he's kneeling. A length of rope is coiled on the floor next to him. "This is how they got out without being noticed. They've gone to report back, and then they'll return here to keep their promise. They've left the rope so that they can be let back in to rescue everyone!" I don't know what to say. One end of the rope is still attached firmly to the bars of the window. It does look as though Sekani is right; someone must have let the spies out and then hidden the rope away neatly inside the room again afterwards. If the spies had fled from Rahab, they'd have had to leave the rope hanging out of the window. The king's men would have found it and known that Rahab had lied to them and they'd be back here arresting us all even now... Perhaps the two men really are protecting us after all.

"Maybe. But what if the spies only said what they did so that Rahab would let them go? What if they're not coming back to help us? We'll be destroyed, Sekani."

"So, we know Jericho is going to be destroyed, and you're not sure whether you believe the spies really are coming back to get us. If that's true and if you're right, then waiting here – doing nothing – is the worst thing we could possibly do."

Deep down inside me I still feel convinced that we should stay, but I can't really explain why any more... I know we could be in serious danger from our own people if they find out what really happened here today. Jericho's army have never exactly looked after slum-dwellers like us before now. Sekani is right; we'd actually be far safer leaving before they do find out. And it sounds like Jericho are just going to hide themselves away behind the wall when Israel arrives. They won't fight back. So we could actually be in less danger outside the wall with them than in our own house. Maybe I have been unfair on Sekani. He certainly has a point. Staying here, we're an easy target for the king's men *and* for Israel. Could it really hurt us to go in search of Israel's spies?

6

"Deliver our lives from death."

Soldiers stand shoulder to shoulder, stretching as far as the eye can see in either direction. Each has a sword raised in his right hand and the same determined expression on his fearless face. Behind the first row stand another, identically posed, and another behind that. As far back as the horizon like rows of barley in the field, the Israelite army stand: united, strong, determined.

Behind Jericho's inner wall, soldiers cower in tiny clusters, clinging to each other and trembling with fear. Some have barricaded themselves inside their homes. Others try to blend in with ordinary citizens. Dotted around the city like seeds on the breeze: scattered, weak, fearful.

I stare out of the window, oblivious to the beauty of the setting sun over the Jordan and smile instead at the fantasy in my mind. I have a promise of protection from the great army of Israel: an army who have escaped Egypt; an army who have overthrown cities. In my mind, I'm now part of this great army. Alongside them, I'm going to expose Jericho's king and all his men for the cowards they really are. Never again will they sneer at me from the wall because I live in the slums. Never again will they insult my family to make themselves feel superior.

I stand in the front line, shoulder to shoulder with Israel's soldiers, a sword raised in my right hand and a determined expression on my fearless face. A shout goes up from behind me. My voice joins the cry. As one with the great army I step forward and we march towards the outer wall of Jericho. The ground trembles with the might of our feet.

The enormous gates swing open before us as my neighbours welcome us in. They are cheering us on: smiling, waving, clapping. The slum-dwellers now stand on the inner walls facing the city, looking down their noses at the king and his men: laughing, mocking, spitting.

Tabia is still standing inside the room with me, but she's not aware of the scene I'm imagining. While I stare from the window, lost in my thoughts, her eyes remain focused intently on the coil of rope at my feet. She is thinking. I don't interrupt her. I know that she will soon realise I'm right. That she may, even now, be working out the finer details of her plan for us to escape. Very soon she'll tell me exactly what I have to do, how, when and why it will work. And then we'll be out, the family will be safe and I will be marching with Israel's infamous army. I allow my mind to drift again into satisfying thoughts of success and glory.

We move effortlessly through the city, swords raised, gathering up the powerless soldiers and surrounding them outside the palace. They have no way out. A deep silence falls over the residents of the slums who are lining the walls to watch. Once more, a united shout goes up from the great army of Israel who stand shoulder to shoulder. The whole, intimidating sound seems to issue from within my very soul. Beneath the power of our angry glare, the soldiers of Jericho melt away into the ground leaving only scarlet pools of blood where they once stood. They are defeated. Victory and Jericho is ours!

Is this how it will happen? Will it be so straightforward? Probably, I tell myself, perhaps even easier. Israel is a great army whose reputation is built on its previous successes. They are known throughout the land before they have even set foot upon our soil. Already, they have intimidated the king of Jericho – a man who lives only to intimidate others. When they arrive, what hope will there be? We have to get out...

"Tabia?" I turn towards her, though my mind is still distracted by my predictions.

The entire army of Jericho turn slowly to face me. The movement is smooth and united. The soldiers are dignified in their strength. I raise my arms high into the air and my army kneels down to bow at my feet. On the walls, the residents of Jericho are cheering for their new king: King Sekani of Jericho.

I smile to myself. "Tabia?"

7

"Tie this cord of scarlet thread in the window."

"Tabia?"

Sekani's voice drifts gently across the room. It breaks my concentration. He has been looking out of the window. I've been lost in my thoughts, reflecting on all that's happened in the past few hours: everything we've overheard, everything Sekani said and all the things we know are going to happen here. Can it really be only this afternoon we were playing tricks on our unsuspecting neighbours? Earlier today that our biggest worry was what our mother would say about the jobs we'd ignored? We've been ripped out from that easy-going life without warning and thrown into a world of scary responsibility. What we do now matters. It will make a difference, one way or the other. We have to get this right. We're not playing any more. I realise that the light from the window is fading fast. Time is moving on.

"Tabia?"

I look up from the coil of rope at last and notice that Sekani has turned to face me. He is waiting for my answer. I have to make a choice. He's looking to me to make the final decision about what we should do.

I nod, avoiding his eyes.

"Tabia, are you sure that you're happy about…?"

Looking straight at him this time, I nod again.

"You're not just doing this because I talked you into it?"

I walk over to the window where Sekani is standing and pick up the rope. I turn the coil around in my hands a few times, letting the loops fall free and creating some slack.

I shake my head.

"So you won't blame me if…?"

"Sekani, you were right. If we stay here and the spies do not come back, then…" I trail off, not wanting to speak the horrible truth aloud.

"Yes, but if we go and—"

"If we go, we have a chance to save ourselves, and at least the possibility of helping our family. There's nothing we can do for anyone by staying here. Nothing."

I hand the coiled end of the rope to my brother and pick up some of the slack from the ground. The rope is rough and worn. Three individual cords have been wrapped firmly around one another. Some of the strands are broken and frayed, but they are held in place by the twisted structure. I take a firm grip with each hand and pull as hard as I can in opposite directions. The rope is strong. The cords support and strengthen one another. I pull harder and my right hand, still clinging tightly, slips along the rope, stinging my palm. I automatically let go.

"Ouch."

Sekani quickly takes over. He checks the knot that attaches the rope to the window. He spends a long time examining it closely while I blow gently onto my sore palm to relieve the burning. Then he takes the rope in both hands and pulls hard against the knot. It holds. He leans back with his weight low to the ground. There's a jolt as the knot slides. I gasp as Sekani's body lurches backwards and he stumbles to keep his balance. He sees my shocked expression and begins to laugh.

"It was pointing out of the window. It twisted round because I was pulling into the room," Sekani explains, sitting down on the floor and dropping the rope. "Don't worry. It's a good knot. It'll hold." My relief must show because Sekani laughs again. "It took the weight of two fully grown men, Tabia. We'll be absolutely fine."

I nod. I want to believe he's right. I look out of the window. It's almost dark now and I can hardly see the ground. I know it's a long way though; a really long way. We're upstairs. The thought of climbing down even to ground level scares me, but our house is built into the wall that defends the city. And that wall is built on the top of another, even bigger wall that stops the whole city sliding down the hill it's built on. That means we have to climb down three or maybe even four times as far as ground level. I shudder at the thought.

"So, shall we leave in the morning?"

"No."

"Tabia, we shouldn't wait too long. If we stay here tomorrow getting things ready, the spies will have travelled too far and we'll never be able to find them."

"I know. I don't think we should wait that long either."

"Then what—"

"I don't think we should wait at all. They've already had a huge head start and…" I pause, unsure whether to admit this. I decide that if we're going to succeed out there, I'm going to need to be totally truthful with my brother. "… and if we wait until morning, I might change my mind. We've got to go now, Sekani."

With both feet resting firmly against the mud-brick wall outside the window, one hand wrapped tightly around the bar and the other clinging desperately to the rope, I take one last look into the room I've just left. Sekani is right there, nodding encouragement, willing me on in his eagerness to follow through the small opening that forms our gateway to the outside world. I take a deep breath, wondering whether this is really the right thing to do. Reminding myself firmly that it's the only option we've got, I tentatively let go of my clasp on the window bar and put my trust fully into the rope from which I hang. I curl my fingers around the cord and wince. This is the hand I injured earlier. The pain is bearable, but it's not going to make my task any easier. I look back to Sekani. As I wonder whether I'm going to survive the climb, I notice another cord tied in the window that I had not seen before: A short red rag that seems utterly out of place. What could it be doing there? Deciding that I am not going to find an answer while dangling six metres above ground level, I shuffle my feet a little further down the wall and begin, cautiously, to descend. I soon find a comfortable rhythm, moving one hand after the other and adjusting my footing. I try to bear most of my weight with my good hand, relying on the less secure grip of the sore palm only long enough to whip the other one past it and grab the rope again.

As my confidence grows, I allow myself to breathe in the cool refreshing night air and enjoy the adrenaline that is pumping through my body. My heart is beating hard and fast but it's not just with fear of falling. I feel a sense of freedom and adventure like nothing I've known before. Outside the house, outside the slums and outside the city wall, I have an incredible new sensation of space. I feel very small compared to the vast darkness that envelops the plains around Jericho, and yet the freedom is exciting. The king's men have barricaded and guarded the city gates, but Sekani and I have escaped! We've found a way out of Jericho and away from certain death. My heart fills with pride. I have a purpose to drive me onwards down this rope. I'm doing something important for people I care about. The sense of achievement overwhelms me and I feel like laughing aloud. We cannot fail! Everything feels so right. We'll find the spies, make a plan and get my family out to safety before the rest of Israel arrives at Jericho's gates.

The wall I'm facing changes from mud brick to stone and I know that I've now reached the section of wall that holds back the embankment. It's odd to think that the wall that I'm now using to steady myself has held the ground in place beneath my home for generations. Every day, I've walked, run and played on the street, not giving a single thought to the wall that held it all in place and now I'm depending on that same wall for my life.

I look up to see Sekani clambering through the window above me and glimpse a fleck of bright red above his head. What's that? I puzzle over it for the next few moments until I remember the short piece of cord I'd seen on my way out. I'm surprised to be able to see it from this distance and that unsettles me a little. The cord is too short to have any useful purpose, but its bright red is extremely eye-catching, even in the gradually thickening darkness. I wish I'd thought to remove it while I'd been up there. I can't help thinking that it draws too much attention to the house. Jericho's men are out here somewhere searching for the spies and the scarlet cord is extremely noticeable. I can't climb back up to get it now though, and Sekani's missed his chance too. He's catching up with me fast. He seems much more at home on the rope than I feel, and is moving more quickly, enjoying the challenge and the freedom. I put the red cord to the back of my mind. There's nothing I can do about it now, and even if the soldiers do see it there in the window it doesn't mean anything. They'll probably just think it's a bit odd, like I did, and forget all about it, which is exactly what I should do.

The rope runs out and I'm still dangling a little way above the ground. I take a deep breath and let go of the rope. Before I know it, my feet touch the ground. As they do, my knees give way. My feet have slid out from underneath me and I land hard on my thigh. My arm hits the ground a couple of seconds later and I partly slide, partly roll a little way down the slope, stirring up a thick cloud of dust as I go. I must have landed on some loose earth. I hurry to my feet and hope that my brother didn't notice. I'm not hurt, but I am embarrassed. I give my clothes a hasty brush down with my grubby hands, then turn to face the immense, dark plains. I stare out into nothingness. I forget everything else and take in the strange sight. I feel numb. Completely unsure of what to do next, I dither on the spot. The spies will be on their way towards the river, but where will Jericho's men be? Will they take the shortest route to the Jordan too, or will they be searching round the walls? In this darkness, we won't have much warning of their approach and we certainly can't afford to be found here. I scan the blackness, wondering what to do for the best. The flat terrain offers us no shelter and we have only the distant rush of water in the Jordan and the fading drone of the city as reference points to navigate by.

Sekani drops the last few feet from the rope behind me with a dull thud and as I look round a truly horrible thought occurs to me. He skids to a halt by my side.

"Sekani, the rope!"

PART TWO: ISRAEL

"A city set on a hill [Jericho] cannot be hidden."

8

"Within three days you are to cross this Jordan."

"Haven't you finished yet?" It's Gurion, my older brother. He loves to tease me. At the moment, he's lying back in the shade of our tent, stretched out with his arms behind his head pretending to be simply enjoying a lazy afternoon. Really he's as alert as a soldier in training, looking for every little chance to let me know how useless I am or how much better he could do something or annoy me in any other way he can. It's his little game to try to get a reaction from me. "My jobs were done hours ago, Daya. What's taking you so long?"

"Haven't you got anything more interesting to do, Gu?"

"Interesting? Here? You are joking? The tents are up; I've collected the water and lit the fire; Dad's at a meeting for officers and Mum's helping the neighbours with their children. There's nothing left for me to do now except relax." I look up from the bowl of manna. He's smirking. I ignore it. "You, on the other hand, my little Daya, still have dinner to prepare and all the beds to make. And I expect after helping with the little ones, Mum will be too tired to wash bowls, so you'll probably be doing those later too."

"You know, if you care so much about me, you could always help."

There's a moment's hesitation, before Gurion retorts, "I could, couldn't I? But then, I have worked hard, and I am very tired, so I probably should just rest here a little while longer."

I smile to myself. Gurion can be lazy and annoying, but he's not very original about it. "All right then, Gu. You rest. You have worked hard. In fact, all this conversation must be very tiring for you too; you should probably stop talking now and try to sleep. It'll do you good."

Gurion smiles. He's letting me have my way and giving me some peace for now, but there'll be another round of teasing later. He'll wait until he detects that I'm hot and tired, then launch another attack. I don't mind though. His brotherly banter is just as much part of my daily life as preparing manna and making beds. It'd be odd if it didn't happen. And I know that when it matters, he'd protect me against anyone. I am his little sister, after all.

Daily life for me is a never-ending stream of setting up and packing away our camp. For as long as I can remember, our tribe, Asher, have been nomadic. My parents hate it when I call it that: "You mustn't say 'nomadic', Daya. It makes us sound like we are simply wandering with no purpose in life. You know that God brought our great nation out of a life of slavery in Egypt, that he brought our ancestors through the Red Sea, defeated great nations, provided food and water in the harshest of conditions and still meets our every need. Have you forgotten who we are? We are Israel! God has promised us a magnificent new home where the land is abundant. We are not nomads, Daya. We are on a momentous journey; part of a historic plan." I've heard it a million times. I can hear their voices now, and see the hurt looks on their faces. That doesn't change the fact that ever since I can remember, we've been going nowhere and the most "momentous" thing I've experienced is the daily fall of manna on the ground. Honestly, I don't even find that as amazing as everyone seems to think I should; the sun rises each morning, there's manna on the ground. What's so special about that? My parents wouldn't be too happy if they heard me say that, but I've never known it any other way. After all, what else would we eat?

Now that Gurion has lost interest in his favourite game of annoying me, I listen to the sounds of the campsite and get back to work. Nearby, I can hear odd little bits of conversation and laughter as neighbours settle down to their mealtimes and chat about the day. Sounds of families relaxing together or helping each other with jobs mingle together as everyone prepares to camp here by the Jordan. The great river growls in the background all the time. The water rushes and crashes as it runs past our camp. I imagine it to be like a terrifying army, charging towards its enemy with a deafening battle cry, tearing up the ground as it goes, stopping for nothing, focused and determined, as I imagine the Egyptians would have been when they chased my grandparents across the desert and through the mountains to the Red Sea. How thrilling to have been there, to be part of such an adventure. Life with God was so exciting then – so different to the life I'm living now.

I've been lost in my daydream of daring escape while pottering around in the tents preparing the beds for tonight and time has quickly passed. I go outside now to check the food and find that Mum has returned and sent Gurion to fetch more water for washing.

"The meal is almost ready," I tell her. "How were the children today?"

"Boisterous as ever. I don't know how their mother copes sometimes. I said I'd go again tomorrow for a few hours to give her a break. Will you be all right here?"

We're interrupted by Dad and Gu arriving back and I don't have a chance to answer. Gurion's loud complaints attract everyone's attention.

"Dad, what's going on? I'm your eldest child – your son – and old enough to know. Why won't you tell me? The other boys always know everything. It's not fair."

"Enough, Gurion. Please pour the water so that we can wash for dinner."

"But—"

My father's look is enough to stop even my brother going any further with his questions, but Gu's already said enough to give away that something out of the ordinary is happening. My mother's face is questioning, but she waits for my father's lead. I busy myself serving the meal, keeping my eyes and ears open for clues. Gurion the Unsubtle plonks himself down by the fire and glares at my father, his arms folded in protest.

My father doesn't speak again until the meal has been served and everyone has taken their turn washing their hands. He's made us all wait and wonder. This must be important. I'm desperate to know now, so I leave my food untouched while I listen.

"Within three days, we will cross the River Jordan and enter the land we have been promised. God has appointed Joshua to lead us. We must gather our supplies and consecrate ourselves."

I look at my father. He is straight-faced and serious. He nods to confirm his own words but doesn't offer any more detail. I look at my mother. She's listened carefully and her eyes are trusting, but she also seems to have a lot of questions to ask. Gurion is staring open-mouthed. He's the first to speak.

"You're joking aren't you, Dad? I know you are. I mean, that's not even possible. Have you seen the river?" He looks at me with an all-knowing look on his face. "Dad's joking. Trust me. It's not true. But there is something going on. What did you really discuss at that meeting, Dad? Stop teasing us and—"

"Gurion." My mother's quiet voice contains a hint of warning. She's still looking at my father.

"What?"

"It's the truth. Your father is not joking."

My father nods again.

Gurion opens his mouth to continue arguing, but fills it with food instead.

"Gurion," says my father. Gu looks up, chewing on his large mouthful. "You were asked to secure the tents. It looks as though a slight breath of wind would bring them down. After dinner you will redo the job – properly this time."

Gurion's cheeks flush red and he looks at the floor. "Yes, Father."

I can't help but smile. Gu was so sure earlier that he'd have the evening off while I slaved away, and now he has to fix the tents with Father watching his every move. He won't be taking any short cuts now.

I collect up the bowls for washing and think about what Dad told us. My mind is spinning as I try to grasp the new information. Like Mum, I believe my father is speaking the truth. But Gu has a good point too; crossing that raging river would be crazy – at least until it stops spilling over its banks!

9

"Great cities fortified to heaven."

This is so unfair! I've done this job once already. I slaved away to put the tents up in the blazing sun this afternoon while Dad sat in the cool shade of a palm tree, chatting to the other officers and listening to their ridiculous suggestions. There's not even a hint of breeze today so I was scorched to the bone while I worked single-handedly. Then, before I could have a drink to cool myself down, I actually had to collect the water by myself too. Daya looks at me as if I'm lazy when I complain, but I'd like to see her putting up a tent. And as if I weren't already hot enough, she wanted me to light a fire so that she could cook.

There is absolutely no chance that these tents would fall down in the night. All right, I may have left a few bits loose here and there, but as I said, there's not even a waft of air from the river reaching us. What could possibly happen? Dad is just making me do this to get me out of his hair because I asked him too many questions. Well, forgive me for trying to taking an interest in what's going on around here!

Usually, life is an endless cycle of putting up tents and hauling water around from place to place. Nothing actually happens, ever. But today, as I slowly recovered from all my hard work, I noticed something going on. People seemed different – restless – like they were expecting something. Women who'd usually rest in their tents before preparing their family meals were gathering in groups to gossip. Children were running from tent to tent with whispered messages. So of course I wanted to know all about it! Most boys my age have fathers who tell them things, especially when they're the eldest child, like me. After all, I'm going to be the one going to those meetings one day, relaying information back to my own family. Shouldn't I be in training or something? When Dad was my age he was trusted with much more than I am. I know he even helped out when there were battles – not fighting, but right there among the action. Does he think I can't handle hearing the plans? *No, Gurion is only good for putting up tents and fetching water. We couldn't possibly tell him anything or let him actually help with anything important, could we?*

So, Daya is gloating now because I have more jobs to do when I thought I'd finished. She hasn't actually said anything yet, but I know she's just waiting for her opportunity. She's washing the bowls from dinner with a smirk on her face. Mum and Dad are too close by for her to make a move, but I know she can't wait to get me back for teasing her earlier. Well, I had worked hard, really hard, and she was only just beginning. She'll soon be finished and I'll still be here, checking every detail to make sure the tents are secure. It's unfair. And if Dad is right, they'll soon be taken down again anyway. It's really unfair.

If Dad is right: If we are going to cross the Jordan this week. That is a big "if". I don't know how he seriously thinks we're going to cross that river. It's fast. And wide. And probably really deep too. People collecting water today were afraid to get close to the edge, and more than one actually lost their grip on their water jugs because the current was stronger than they thought. The jugs disappeared downstream in seconds, or got crushed into little pieces by debris under the surface. Our fully grown men would be swept away by the flow, so how we're supposed to get the women and children across, and all the equipment, I don't know. He's mad!

I think Mum has had the same thought actually, because Dad is talking to her now while he thinks that Daya and I are too busy to notice. Am I busy? Well, I'm pretending to be. But I'm keeping a very close eye on what's going on outside. Mum looks really worried. Dad doesn't though, so there's obviously some sort of plan in place. Let's just hope it's a good one. I'm going to move to the entrance of the tent now to see if I can hear them any better – I'll pretend to be adjusting one of the knots there.

"Joshua?" my mum is muttering in disbelief.

"Yes, God has appointed Joshua to lead us." Dad puts a reassuring hand on her shoulder. "Don't forget that Joshua worked closely with Moses for a long time. And before Moses died, he laid hands on him. Joshua is wise. He'll lead us well."

A vague memory stirs in my mind from a story my father once told us about the battle at Rephidim. *Didn't Joshua lead the army then?* Any man who can command an army to victory like that has to be a good choice for a leader now.

"Like he led us against the Amalekites?" The words spill out of my mouth before I remember that I'm not supposed to be listening to my parents' conversation.

My father looks up. I duck back into the tent and busy myself tidying away rope ends.

"Gurion?" he calls after me.

Oops! Why do words always come spewing out of my mouth before I have chance to think? Sometimes I wish I was actually a bit quieter, like Daya. I peer cautiously out at the darkening evening and the shadowy faces of my parents, dreading what's coming. But I don't need to worry; they're smiling.

"You're right, Gurion," he says. "That was Joshua. Come and sit by the fire and I'll tell you about it. You've done enough work for one day. You too Daya."

I don't need telling twice. The fire isn't burning fiercely any more. It's dimmed to a pretty feeble glow now, but it's enough to light my father's face as he settles into storytelling mode. Daya sits opposite him, and I make myself comfortable a little off to one side. Experience tells me that I can get away with daydreaming better that way, and I don't really want to listen anyway. I'm tired, I've heard the story before and I'd actually much rather hear about the plan for getting us across that river. I just can't figure out how it can be possible.

I'm still tackling this frustrating problem when I realise that Dad has moved on. My ears prick up at the mention of the river. "... and beyond the Jordan are great cities: prosperous cities with land that produce plentiful harvests and have water to spare; cities with goods to trade and business for their people; cities with walls, fortified and strong, defended by rich kings with powerful armies."

I hear my sister breathe in and see her eyes widen a little at the thought of such a place. I smile to myself. Daya loves my father's stories. Her imagination thrives on every detail of the people and places he describes, especially when they're so different from our own way of life. I'm not so easily satisfied though. I still have too many questions and I can't help thinking that this story of the cities beyond the Jordan will actually turn out to be no more real to us than the stories of Israel's distant past. They're great stories, but that's all they are – stories. We're not going to get across that river, and even if we do, it won't be nearly as exciting as Dad pretends in his folk tales. Don't get me wrong. I'd love to be part of an adventure like the ones he tells us. I just don't think it'll happen, so there's no point hoping and pretending it will. Dad doesn't even trust me enough to tell me about the plans they made at the meeting. That means there's no way he'll trust me with anything important if Joshua really does have a way of getting us all across to these "great" cities. *Gurion can't be trusted. Don't let Gurion help.* So while they're actually having an adventure, creating new stories for Daya to tell her children one day, I'll be left to pack away the tent, or carry the equipment, or deliver some pathetic message for him.

Or maybe not. Because this time Gu is not going to sit around and wait for his father to tell him what to do. This time Gu is going to be part of the action and prove them all wrong – show them what he's capable of. That's what I'll do. I will. I'll make my own decisions; plan my own way into the action – make a story of my very own!

10

"All Israel crossed on dry ground."

Israel was on the move again. The nation was used to upheaval and the whole procedure was running as smoothly as Pharaoh's ships on the waters of the Nile. It was the tenth day of the first month, exactly 40 years since Israel had chosen lambs to slaughter and prepared to leave Egypt. Then, they had organised themselves by family, tribe and military group so that each individual knew where they belonged as they followed the swirling mass of cloud in the day and the blazing glow of fire at night. Forty years on, the system remained unchanged as Joshua prepared to move the nation of Israel into the land that God had promised them.

Earlier that morning, beside the powerful and untamed waters of the Jordan River, the fiercely flickering tongues of flame had gradually dimmed down to be slowly replaced by willowy soft waves of wispy cloud above the tabernacle. Day was dawning. The camp of Judah faced east and its inhabitants were the first to see the sunrise, just as they would be the first to set out once more towards their promised goal when the cloud lifted. The camp of Dan was located to the north and that of Reuben to the south, each with their tribes and family groupings arranged neatly around their standards. These colourful fabric banners provided visual reference points to keep order within the vast mass of people. Any individual could easily locate their family, using the standards as a guide. From the tabernacle at the centre of the camp, the four largest standards of the military groupings were clearly visible, one on each side. Behind each of those stood three smaller standards, indicating the positions of the tribes that belonged to that military group, and many smaller banners showed where each family had their camp within each tribe. To the west of the tabernacle was the standard of Dan; and behind it the three smaller standards of the tribes, Dan, Asher and Naphtali.

Near to Asher's standard, Gurion, Daya and their parents had slept. The tents that Gurion had secured three days ago provided basic shelter for the family from the extreme heat during the day and cold nights. Outside, a small collection of stoneware stacked neatly beside the embers of last night's fire was all that the family needed to gather water and prepare meals. The clothes that Daya had washed by hand in water from the Jordan River hung from lengths of cord between the tents, ready for today's important journey. The family did not possess much. This was normal for the families that made up the tribes and nation of Israel. Whenever the pillar of fire or column of cloud had lifted from above the tabernacle, Israel had packed up camp and followed where God led them. Everything they owned had to be moved too, so extra belongings were an unnecessary burden. And the land where Israel had journeyed for so long had been barren and desolate; it had not provided luxuries of any description. Much of the time it had not even met the Israelites' most basic needs – God had done that. He had provided miracle after miracle so that his people would learn to trust him.

Now, the sun was climbing and the temperature was quickly rising. The tribes of Israel were standing in formation, waiting for the command from Joshua. They were watching the swift surging of the water ahead of them as it journeyed towards the sea of death. Their focus was held by the rays of the rising sun as they fell on the frothy white tips of the rapids. The hordes were silent as every member of each tribe questioned their chances of survival in the turbulent waters of the Jordan. The lessons of the past 40 years – the knowledge of God's miraculous provision and the promises he had given Israel were entirely forgotten in the face of the terrifying danger they were now confronting.

Towards the back of the crowd though, something was happening. First, one pair of eyes turned tentatively away from the water to take in this new sight. Then others close by looked round too. Soon, people were nudging their neighbours or nodding their heads in the direction of the 12 men until all eyes were fixed on their every footstep. Still nobody spoke. They watched as the 12 priests walked slowly and deliberately past the tribes. They saw 12 pairs of hands supporting two long, golden poles above the priests' heads. They saw the beautifully crafted golden box secured to the poles by four golden rings on its feet. Without a sound, Israel watched the ark proceed towards the Jordan River and knew again the presence of their God. Joshua was responsible for organising the people of Israel to carry out God's instructions, but this was not Joshua's plan. God was taking Israel into the land he had promised them; and God was conspicuously leading the way.

The 12 priests approached the edge of the floodwaters. Israel had walked behind in silence for the mile or so from the camp to the river. They had kept their distance from the ark as Joshua had instructed them so that they were able to see it clearly at all times and follow its direction. Now they stopped walking and watched. The priests stepped into the overflow of the Jordan. Their feet disappeared from view beneath the surface. And then they stopped. They stood absolutely still in the shallow edge, water swirling around their ankles, still bearing the golden ark above their heads, and they waited.

The nation of Israel held its breath, watching and waiting as the priests stood still. The 12 did not stride any further into the Jordan nor retreat to dry land. They simply stood.

As Israel waited, the water level began to fall. The change was hardly noticeable at first, but the tops of the priests' feet emerged above the surface once more. They had not moved from the place where they had come to rest. Water continued to flow away downstream, but the quantity of water arriving at the place where Israel watched was quickly diminishing. The soles of the priests' feet were soon visible again and the water's edge receded until it was no longer overflowing the riverbanks. And the level continued to fall, exposing more and more of the jungle-like undergrowth in the riverbed. Ground that had been waterlogged dried rapidly in the powerful heat of the sun.

Upstream, something even more incredible was happening. Far in the distance, in a gorge between lofty cliffs, water was coming to a standstill as if blocked or barricaded. The level was rising so that a great wall of water built up high above the normal level of the Jordan. Soon, the river was completely cut off there and nothing more flowed down to where the priests stood. Israel watched the last trickle wind away past them, twisting and turning on its path downstream, leaving the ground arid and the undergrowth parched and wilting.

The nation of Israel looked across the dry bed of the River Jordan. Directly in front of them stood the land that they had been promised long ago. In stark contrast to the primitive campgrounds they had so often constructed in the dry and uninhabited wilderness, they saw vast plains with palm trees and rich, green vegetation: vines and fig trees and strange red fruits; fields of wheat and barley and springs of water that nourished the crops. Beyond the plains towered the great metropolis of Jericho, set high on an embankment with imposing stone walls that seemed to reach to the skies. And now nothing stood between Israel and Jericho's city gates.

11

"The waters of the Jordan returned to their place."

I'm back in the camp with my family again. I'm pretty cross about that actually, but there's nothing else I could have done. I set out early and got away before Dad could share out the jobs – otherwise known as leaving all the hard work to me. He likes to keep me busy, or out of trouble as he sees it. Well, this morning I didn't even give him a chance. Before the sun had risen, I was gone.

I tried to get Daya to come with me, but I didn't have much chance to properly explain what I was thinking. I thought, since she likes Dad's stories so much, she might like to come with me and create one of our own. I also thought, and this was pretty clever actually, that because Daya is much more careful than I am she'd be pretty useful to have around. And I figured it'd be pretty boring on my own anyway. So, I did try to talk to her last night before we went to bed, but Daya's head was full of Dad's latest story and planning for today and she didn't really listen to her silly old brother. You'd think she'd have been interested to know how I'd solved the biggest problem that faced Joshua: crossing the powerful Jordan. But no! And this morning, I tried again, but Daya was being all dutiful about the jobs she'd been given to do – something to do with washed clothes – and about how Mum would be busy helping with the neighbour's children and would be relying on her.

Actually, Mum and Dad are always relying on us. That's the whole point. They're never here but they always expect us to be. They get the excitement and we get the chores. That's why I want to mix things up a little. I was going in search of excitement and a story to tell, and leaving the jobs to them. Not that it was going to be easy. This was probably going to be the hardest day's work of my life. Building anything is tiring, and it's not as though I'm an expert. I mean, I'm good at tents, but...

I'd decided the extra effort would be worth it though, when I was explaining to the officers at the end of the day how I'd thought up my plan and carried it out. Daya still wasn't listening to reason, so I left her behind. It was a shame to set out on my own, but better than hearing her lectures all day about what I should've been doing. What a man my age should be doing is getting involved, making a difference – and that is exactly what I was planning to do as I crept away from the camp before daybreak. Because of me, Jericho would soon be within our reach.

I heaved the makeshift sack further up onto my back and trudged on. It was heavy, but I had to get away from Asher and find myself a spot near the river to work. I passed several people who were on their way back to the camp with water jugs. Most gave me funny looks. I let them. Genius is rarely understood, but they'd be thanking me later. I stopped one or two lads of about my age to try and recruit them, but the first one didn't even stop to listen – very rude – and the other just laughed. Fine. He obviously didn't see the brilliance of my plan. It didn't matter anyway.

With relief, I dropped my bundle under a tree that grew beside the overflowing river and wiped the sweat off my forehead. I untied the rope that was securing the cloth of my tent around its contents and spread everything out on top of it. If people wouldn't listen, perhaps they'd believe me when they saw my plan in action. Not wasting another minute, I set to work.

The first part was surprisingly easy. The parts that usually made up my tent were suited perfectly to their new roles. I set the longer posts out against each other, side by side, with the shorter ones lying across them at each end. I also added one diagonally across to give extra support. Then, I used the various lengths of rope to lash the posts securely together. I pulled and twisted and knotted and cut until the structure was complete. And I was pleased. I looked around to see if anyone would comment, but everyone in the tribe in the nearest part of the camp was too busy to notice. Never mind. I already knew I'd done a good job. I didn't need anyone else to tell me that.

I flipped the structure over, so the flat surface was on top, and walked across it. It seemed secure. Then I pushed, stamped and jumped on it too. It held firm. Excellent! I was confident that this first trial section was up to the task. Being wood, it would float easily and once I'd secured it to the bank, I'd be able to convince a few more people to help with the construction. I looked across the water. It was a long way, probably half a mile or more. I was going to need a lot more sections like this one. Still, I could worry about that later.

I set to work again, securing long pieces of rope firmly to two corners of my platform. I trailed one across the ground to the tree, wound it round the trunk several times and used every knot I knew to make perfectly sure it wouldn't budge. I repeated this with the other length of rope and another tree slightly further downstream. *The moment of truth...* I went back to the edge of the Jordan, lined myself up halfway between the two trees and gently nudged my creation into the very edge of the water. I watched. The wooden square was swept fast in one direction by the current. There was a jolt as it reached the end of the slack in the rope and lurched backwards. The water carried on flowing around and under it and it tipped violently, dipping below the surface. But it bobbed up again, wobbled a little and then steadied itself. *Good.* I tested it with a toe. It felt strong. So, I put one foot on to its now slightly slippery surface and steadied myself. *Fine.* I slowly leant forwards, moving my weight onto the structure. I felt it sink a little, but not significantly. *Success!* I jumped back onto the bank. I knew I should really check that it would take my whole weight, but I thought I'd save that moment of glory for when I had some witnesses to appreciate it with me.

Excitedly, I spun around to face the campground. I was convinced now that I'd found the answer. I had thought of everything. We'd create many more, possibly even hundreds, of platforms like mine, lash them all together in a long chain and throw the whole thing into the river. We'd leave anchoring ropes attached to every third or fourth section which would be held by great teams of strong men on the banks. When my pathway had settled down into its position on top of the water, I would stroll across and secure it firmly to the opposite bank. Then, I'd wave a signal to Joshua, who'd direct each family of every tribe and military group across until the whole of Israel had crossed the Jordan. I'd shake their hands and accept their thanks as they arrived safely in the Promised Land. By tonight, I'd be a national hero. All I had to do now was recruit a team and inform the officers of the plan. And I was more than ready to get on with it. I couldn't wait.

But I was horrified by the sight that met my eyes when I turned around. The campground was deserted. Totally empty. Completely abandoned. The tribe that had been busily working behind me had gone. Gone! And I hadn't even noticed. All that lay in front of me now was a large area of flat, empty ground without a trace of human presence. I hurried towards it. I had to find them quickly. Panic was making my heart pound. I should have got to the officers sooner. I hoped that they weren't thinking of doing anything silly. Hoped that they had realised they needed someone with a plan. Hoped that they were waiting for me to arrive…

After that moment, it was all a bit disappointing. The excitement gradually turned to defeat. In my plans, I'd proved Dad wrong; Gurion the Great had been trustworthy and valuable; he'd got right into the heart of the action with Israel's men. He'd made decisions, taken control, commanded men, directed women and been a hero to children. Gurion had solved the problem, found the answer and guided a nation to their goal. Gurion had proved himself great and would feature in the stories of generations to come… But it didn't turn out quite that way after all.

•

The tribes were packed up and on their way to the Jordan. Talk about efficient. By the time I got back to Asher they were already lined up with the other tribes, facing the water. Mum frowned at me as I moved towards her and Dad was nowhere to be seen, so I decided to get closer to the front of the procession. I elbowed my way through the crowds ignoring the protests. I was sure the officers must be together near the front, worrying about the water and wondering what to do. And I was right. I could see them. They'd gathered in a circle. But I couldn't get to them quickly enough. The priests were carrying the ark towards the Jordan, and I was forced to stand still and watch silently as they passed. I made myself wait on the spot, not moving a muscle, but inside I was hopping up and down, eager to get going again. I felt like shouting out to the priests that there was no point moving the ark yet. I wasn't ready for them. But knowing I was like a single grain of sand in the vast desert, I decided against it. There were thousands of them, and only one of me.

The priests didn't slow as they neared the water. They didn't stop to speak to the officers. They simply carried on. They were going to go in! Panicking, I set off at a run towards the place where I'd left my great invention. I was never going to get the officers to it in time to prevent the priests, but maybe I could still get it to them.

I ran harder than I'd ever run before. I was sweating by the time I reached the first tree. I ripped and tore at the rope, battling against my own knots to free it. But it was taking too long. I followed the rope along the ground to the wood. I'd untie this end instead and... But I stopped in my tracks. I stared, not believing my eyes. The platform was sitting on the ground. Solid ground. I'd definitely left it in the water. I bent down and saw traces of damp around its edges. But the first lapping ripples of the Jordan were a few metres away. *That's odd.* I pushed the platform towards it with my toe, but it didn't budge. The rope was taut. *What happened? How is that possible?* I was baffled. Still feeling that something wasn't right, I untied the rope from the two corners and picked up the platform. I stood and glanced back at the water. It was now slightly further away. I was sure of it. I didn't have time to worry about that now though. Israel needed me. With the structure wedged awkwardly under my arm, I set off at my fastest walking pace to find the officers. Perhaps the priests had seen sense and waited. Perhaps…

I was distracted from my thoughts by what I could see out of the corner of my eye. The water was receding. In fact, the sun was drying out the land all the way to the actual riverbed. Until now, the water had drenched the land around it, but not now. I could see the banks for the first time. I hesitated. I was anxious to reach Joshua, but the sight of the water visibly receding baffled me. A thought entered my mind. *Would my plan still work?* I forced the thought out and picked up my pace.

But I was too late. My work had been wasted. By the time I'd returned the water was gone and Israel was moving. My brilliant plan was not required any more. The river was there one minute, dangerous and frightening, and then it wasn't. My wooden platform was useless in the parched base of the Jordan. Nobody needed help walking across a dry riverbed, even with the obstacle of the plant life that was uncovered; they all just followed the priests across safely. Boring really. Not quite the story of a lifetime that I'd hoped for. There was nothing else for me to do except take my place in Asher and walk. And I did.

So I'm back home and being left out once again. My parents don't seem to want to talk about where I was, or wasn't, today. They don't realise the lengths I went to to help. Nobody knows. Nobody asked. They're just not involving me in anything now. Actually, I don't mind that. All that's happening anyway is that 12 men are arranging stones to form some sort of monument to our crossing place. One from each tribe was sent to bring a stone from the bed of the River Jordan before the priests finally came out and the water surged back into place. Everyone else is far too interested if you ask me. What's the point? What we should be doing now is thinking about what's next – that fantastic city on the horizon – and how we're going to get past those mega-walls, not dwelling on what we've already done.

But I'm forgetting, silly Gu, that's what Israel are best at – dwelling on stories of the past and letting the future plan itself. That's why it took us so long to get here in the first place, if you ask me. No one else seems to realise that. But then I am quite different. And I won't give up just because one plan failed. That's why I'm going to be great in Israel. I'm going to prove it and make my father proud of me. As soon as I can make my escape again I'm going to go and survey the situation; I'll find out exactly what we're up against and make a new plan. An even better plan. Then, when Joshua falters, Gurion will step in and save the nation! I can make a difference. And I will!

12

"Make flint knives."

"Daya," Gu hisses at me from behind the tent. "Are you on your own?" My brother has been avoiding our parents for the past couple of days – ever since he went off to prove himself. He knows that they're not happy with him for losing a tent and leaving me to pack up the camp by myself. And I'm still annoyed about it too.

"What is it, Gurion?"

"I need to talk to you. Are you alone?"

I shrug. "Yes. Dad's down at the riverbank with the other men…"

"What are they doing there?"

"They've gone to—"

"Never mind. Listen, Daya, I need you to come with me."

"Gurion, if you're trying to get me to come on some crazy mission with you again, the answer is no. I have work to do here." He's not helping my bad mood by going on about this when he already knows how we all feel.

"You'll always have jobs to do, Daya. But you're missing out. I'm telling you, the real adventure is waiting for us over there." He's pointing to the walled city on the horizon.

"Gurion, I have to be honest with you." I sigh heavily, trying to put this the best way I can. "I think you're missing the point. Our whole nation just crossed a raging river on dry ground. Everyone is still talking about it. They've even built a monument to celebrate it. This is big! How much more adventure do you need?"

"It wasn't actually that great though was it, Daya? I mean we all just packed up, walked across and then camped again. That's not really any different from normal, is it?"

He's being really awkward. "Well, some of us packed up. Some of us were nowhere to be seen. But you just don't want to see it, do you? That river is in flood. It shouldn't be possible to cross it at all – you said so yourself. The water stopped flowing at the exact moment that the priests stood in it, and started again at the exact moment they stepped out. That's not normal."

"But it's just another story about Israel, Daya. I want a story about me. I want to be a real part of it. I want to be able to tell my children that I made a difference. Don't you want that, Daya?"

"Gu, I am making a difference. I belong here in the camp, helping with the meals and the washing and—"

"Making a difference?"

"It's not all about big, dramatic gestures that get you noticed. I'm helping to keep our family organised and ready to move when we're asked to. And I'm reliable. I don't just wander off and leave—"

"Hey: That's not fair!"

"No, Gurion. What's not fair is you deciding that you're too important to join in. If more people did that, half the families of Asher wouldn't have been ready to cross. Our tribe wouldn't have taken its place and perhaps we wouldn't be here at all. And what kind of story would that be? We'd all be telling our children how most of Israel went across the Jordan and left us behind because our tents weren't packed up in time."

Gurion has stepped out from behind the tent and moved a lot closer to where I'm sitting. He's staring at me, one eyebrow raised, but I'm not going to be put off by that and he doesn't speak so I carry on. "If you want Dad to trust you and tell you what's happening, you need to show him that you can be trusted. Do whatever he asks you to do. Do it well, however small and pointless it seems, then he'll see that you can handle responsibility and—"

"That's nonsense, Daya. It doesn't matter whether I do those things or not. I'm not a boy anymore – I want to be involved."

"Then why aren't you collecting pieces of flint from the riverbanks with the other men, or knapping them into knives?"

"Is that what...? Why are they...? I didn't know that was..."

"Perhaps if you'd been here."

"That's irrelevant. I don't know why they're wasting their time making little knives when there's a city over there with huge stone walls. They should be there now, finding out everything they can so they can plan a proper strategy. If I were Joshua—"

"But you're not, Gu."

"Well, maybe when he fails because he wasted time making knives that don't stand a chance in a proper battle, I'll be able to step in with a better plan. One based on facts. I'm going to find out exactly what we're up against. Are you with me or not, Daya? It's your last chance."

I laugh. I can't help myself. I still can't believe that he thinks he knows better than the officers of Israel. And he's totally misunderstood what the men are preparing for. "No, Gurion. I'm not coming with you. Joshua is an experienced leader – he knows what he's doing. The knives are not meant for the battle, they're—" But my words are wasted. Gu hasn't waited to find out. He's jumped to his own conclusions and stormed off towards the vast fields of barley. He's so focused on finding his own adventure that he's missing the one happening in his own campground. I sigh and set off quickly after him. I need to get him back before he misses the biggest opportunity of his life.

Chapter 13

"The children whom he raised up in their place."

So, I'm on my own again. I seem to be the only one in the whole of Israel with any common sense left anyway. Daya was talking complete rubbish about how doing all those little tasks around the campsite is actually changing the destiny of the entire nation. Mum and Dad have managed to convince her that she's being valuable. And she loves to hear that. It's a pity for them that I don't believe a word of it. Daya was actually sounding so much like them that I couldn't stand to listen to her any more. I used to think that we were quite similar deep down, but apparently not.

Anyway, I'm going to scout out Jericho with or without my sister's help. After this, I'll be able to provide Joshua's army with information that will make the crucial difference to their battle plan; the difference between actually taking the city and dying a horrible death on day one. I'm going to find out exactly how big the army in Jericho is, what weapons they have, where they'll be waiting and what defences they've already got in place. I've worked out how to do it. It's not actually that hard. There are a lot of trees around the city: mostly sycamore figs and palms. The sycamores are easy to climb and the leaves are thick enough to hide me in their branches. I'm going to listen to the men working in the fields to see what I can find out. Then, I'm going to follow them back in through the gates to get a closer look. If I can report back to Joshua about the inside of the city, he's bound to recruit me to help him with his strategy. Then nobody will be able to tell the story of Jericho without commenting on Gurion's bravery and intelligence. I'll be admired and appreciated by the whole of Israel – and Dad will have to admit that I'm not totally useless. I can't wait!

There's no sign of anybody here so far, but I'll just have to get closer to those walls. I'm keeping a straight path between two barley fields. The stalks are tall enough to keep me hidden from view and I'm heading straight for a sycamore fig that overlooks these fields and a couple more beyond. I'll also have a quick escape route back to camp if I do run into any trouble. I'm feeling quite calm and in control at the moment, but I can feel my heartbeat pulsing heavily through my body. It's almost as though I can hear it. The experience is quite strange and makes me realise how unnaturally quiet everything else is. It's much too quiet. I speed up towards that tree so that I can find out exactly what's going on.

"Gu," hisses a voice from behind me. It startles me. I hadn't been aware of anyone nearby. In fact, I'd thought I was totally alone. I glance back over my shoulder. *Oh great! That's just what I need.* It's Daya. She's been following me. I really don't want to hear anything she has to say so I ignore her and carry on even faster, towards my lookout. "Gu, wait!" I don't. "Gurion!"

"Shhh, Daya!" I growl as I spin around. My eyes have narrowed and I scowl at her. She's going to spoil everything by making so much noise.

"You've got to come back," she says calmly, catching up some ground. "Let me explain what's—"

"No, Daya. I'm going ahead with my plan. You weren't interested, so go back and leave me alone." She doesn't respond, but keeps walking towards me. "Daya, go back. You're spoiling—" I stop because I've heard something. I hold up a hand to warn Daya to be quiet too and, thankfully, she takes the hint. She stops walking and waits for my lead. Yes. I definitely heard footsteps, and now there are faint voices too. They're not very far off, but we have a bit of time. I gesture to Daya to come quietly and she does. We creep as quickly as we dare towards the tree. I swing a leg up over the lowest branch and haul myself up before offering Daya my hand. She hesitates, but I don't know what other option we have. She seems to realise this too, because eventually she takes my hand and scrambles up to join me. We cautiously climb a few more branches until I'm sure we're hidden from view by the closely packed leaves of the sycamore.

"They're circumcising all the men," Daya whispers, getting straight to the point. Suddenly, I'm listening to her. I wasn't expecting that.

A feeble "What?" is all I manage in response.

"To prepare them for battle. As a sign of the promise God made to our people. It's what the knives are for."

"I don't—"

"Just like the men of Israel used to be, when all the exciting things happened after Egypt. You must have heard Dad talk about it?"

"Maybe, but—"

"It means that something's going to happen again. Not just walking around behind the tabernacle, but..."

"Shhh." The voices are getting nearer. I slowly push a branch aside and peer out of the tree to get a better view. I can't work out where the sounds are coming from.

Daya lowers her voice but carries on. "... but real adventure. You're out here looking for an adventure..." I frown at her. "... when it's all happening without you back at the camp." I finally catch sight of the figures I've been looking for. What I see confuses me even more than Daya's news. The figures are not what I expected to see. "You should be there, Gurion."

"Look." I pull Daya closer and point to the two small figures below us, approaching the tree. "You have to be quiet. They'll hear us. We can't go anywhere until they've passed. Just be quiet and listen. They might say something useful." Daya nods. She doesn't have much choice.

I watch in amazement as a boy and a girl get closer to the tree where I'm hiding. What are they doing out here? I was expecting to see men: workers in the field, or soldiers patrolling. So far, the only sign that Jericho is not totally abandoned is these two children. They're younger than me, around Daya's age I'd say. I doubt they'll have anything to say that's worth listening to. I lean back against a thick branch and think. Daya's words start to sink slowly into my mind. *Is she saying what I think she is? What if she's right? Could she be?* There's been no chance to gather any information here today, and meanwhile I'm possibly missing out on my chance to fight for Israel. Maybe I should think about going back. If she is right, I might actually get to be involved in something important for once and if she's not... If she's not right, I can always come back tomorrow and carry on – the workers might be in the fields again by then. After all, it's late now for them to be out – and I could leave Daya behind tomorrow. She talks too much. She'd get us caught. She's too much of a risk.

I smile. I'm pleased with the decision I've made and I lean forward to check where the two children have got to. Once they've safely passed, I can risk climbing down and making my way back. That's odd. I scan around. I've temporarily lost sight of the pair. I look again and my eyes widen as I realise where they are. *This can't be happening!* I blink, but the scene doesn't change. The girl has stopped beneath us, in the shade of the very tree where I'm hiding. And the boy seems to be setting up some kind of basic shelter. They're thinking of staying here! Now there's no chance of getting down from here without being seen. I look out into the surroundings and realise that it is much later than I'd thought. The light is fading, leaving a purple glow on the horizon. They'll camp here until morning! What are we going to do now?

PART THREE: THE PROMISED LAND

"No one went out and no one came in."

14

"The pursuers had sought them all along the road..."

"Tabia, are you awake?" I whisper. She hides her face in her arm and ignores me.

"Tabia!" I try again. I've been awake for a while and I'm fairly certain that we're being watched. The warm sun is rising and the air is perfectly calm. Everything is still. Even the sound of the Jordan is just a gentle hum in the distance. But I'm sure that I heard something a moment ago. As I lay awake, watching the light streaming through the leaves above me, I heard a rustling nearby. I stay still, wondering what to do next. There it is again! I didn't imagine it. But where is it coming from? And what's making the sound? There's absolutely no breeze today, so it can't have been the wind. I look around. A few large birds are circling around above the crops, quickly swooping down and then soaring slowly back up. They're too agile to have made such a disruption. I wonder whether it was an animal in the fields. If it was, there's no sign of any movement there now. Is it possible there's another human close by? But where? I can't be sure where the sound came from. Everything is quiet again now. But it was definitely much closer than I'd like. I'm not sure we're safe.

"Tabia," I say, shaking her gently. "You've got to wake up." She groans.

"Go away, Sekani. It's early."

"We're in danger. I think there's someone else here." That gets her attention. My sister scrambles to sit up, rubbing her eyes, scanning around for some sign of the threat. Only when she is sure that there's no need to immediately run, Tabia leans closer and speaks in a low voice.

"What's going on, Sekani?"

"I thought I heard someone nearby. There was a rustling. I'm not sure where exactly, but it wasn't far away."

"Are you sure? The soldiers have gone back to the city. The fields have been deserted for days. It was probably just—"

"We're not alone, Tabia."

We sit under the sycamore fig, as still as we can, leaning against the trunk and listening for any further sign of movement; any sound that seems out of place. There's nothing.

We've spent several days searching for the two Israelite men who visited our aunt. Frustratingly there's been no sign of them at all and we're both tired from sleeping on rough ground, often in shifts, and from being always alert. Still, I didn't think I was tired enough to start imagining things. I keep listening, but there's nothing to hear and my mind wanders a little.

We knew that the men couldn't have got very far before we set off after them. We also quickly realised that we weren't the only ones looking for them. The king's men had taken my aunt's advice and pursued them from the gate. We soon learned how to keep ourselves hidden in the fields. It wasn't as easy as hiding out in the slums where we know every short cut, hideaway and obstacle, but the principles are the same and the crops do provide pretty good cover. You can't even be heard if you move slowly and carefully enough through them. There are also many trees, providing shelter from the heat. Tabia realised that they give great views over the land too so we could keep track of exactly where the soldiers were, and look out for the missing Israelites without being spotted. The soldiers mostly stuck to the main road anyway. They went as far as the banks of the Jordan and then turned around and headed back towards the city. We haven't given up that easily, but then perhaps we have more to lose.

Unfortunately, we haven't been any more successful in tracking down the Israelite men and I've totally lost track of how long we've spent searching. They'll have to pass us to access the river though. Unless they've crossed already - but how?

There's been no sound or movement nearby and Tabia's beginning to get restless. I'm not sure she believes there was a sound at all because she keeps looking at me sideways. I'm beginning to doubt it myself, but I think it is best to be absolutely certain. I put a finger to my lips and focus hard on listening. The sound could only have come from the crops, but we're surrounded by fields on all sides, so I'm not sure where to concentrate my attention first.

Tabia has settled back against the tree and taken up her task again. Actually, I'm quite proud of my sister. She had huge doubts about coming on this mission, but she's been great at it. She never stops. She's always working out where the men might be, and planning ways to find them. That's why we're staying so close to the river, because she says they'll have to come this way eventually. Tabia is great with strategies, but she trusts my instincts when it comes to keeping a low profile, like now. Avoiding danger is my strength – I've had enough experience of it! We make a great team. She hasn't once suggested giving up and returning home. She believes as strongly as I do that we are our family's only hope.

Finally, I decide that the threat has now passed – if there ever was one at all. I get to my feet and stretch.

"Sorry, I really thought we were being watched."

"Well, you were right to make sure."

"So, what's for breakfast?" I yawn and stretch out again. Sleeping on the ground out here leaves me feeling stiff every morning. It's annoying. Tabia doesn't answer. Her face is still crumpled in thought. I've worried her. "If there was somebody here, Tabia, they've obviously left again. I don't think anyone's realised we're here or we'd know about it by now!"

"Still, if there was somebody close by, I want to know who it was," says Tabia, still ignoring my request for food. "It might have been the two men," she adds. "If they thought there was someone nearby, they'd have been careful to keep quiet. Especially if they thought we were soldiers."

I laugh. "We hardly look like it, Tabia."

"But they may not have seen us either - just heard us close by." She has a point. "I'm going to climb up here, just to make absolutely sure there was nobody. And anyway, it'd be sensible to check that the soldiers are still heading back towards the city before we plan today. Give me a hand, Sekani."

I nod my agreement. Being sensible seems to come so naturally to my sister, I sometimes think she reached adulthood soon after her third birthday. I kneel down and clasp my hands together to give Tabia a foothold, then boost her up so that she can reach the lowest branch.

"Are you all right?" I ask.

"Yes, I've got it," she replies, hauling herself up to sit on the limb. "I'll manage from here. Just keep an eye out."

I turn around to keep watch on the ground as Tabia disappears higher up the tree to get a better view.

15

"… but had not found them."

One last look down confirms that Sekani is watching for signs of movement on the ground. I reach out an arm to grab the branch above. It's just out of reach, so I stand on tiptoes and try again. Stretching until my sides hurt, I grasp each side and walk my feet up the trunk. I'm grateful that the rope burn on my hand has healed because I'm relying on a very tight hold to support my weight. I hold my breath to concentrate. I should be used to all the climbing by now, but I still hate it. When I'm close enough, I wrap one arm tightly over the branch and swing my legs up. One of them lands on target. The other dangles awkwardly beneath me. With a deep breath, I adjust my grasp and use the new foothold to heave the rest of my body up. I shudder, thinking how little there is to support me and I'm glad Sekani's not here to see how pathetic I'm being. I really should be more used to this by now.

I rest for a moment face down with my cheek pressed against the branch and notice that Sekani has wandered round the other side of the tree. He's checking in all directions for danger. Good. I'm grateful he guards so carefully; it means

I can just concentrate on climbing, which I still find annoyingly difficult. Really, it'd be much easier for Sekani to scramble up here and check the view over the plains; he's by far the better climber. But there's a very good reason why I'm here and he's not.

On our first day outside the walls, I was on guard while Sekani climbed a palm. Jericho's soldiers suddenly came into view. I hadn't heard them coming and they were far too close. I panicked and tried to climb up to warn Sekani, but I lost my grip, slipped down and landed hard on my side. I'm sure the soldiers heard my yelp, because they stopped patrolling and stood rooted to the spot. They were listening for another sound. I managed to half-crawl, half-slither away into the cover of the wheat crop without being heard and waited there until they gave up and left. Fortunately for us, Sekani had spotted exactly what was going on. He stayed perfectly quiet too and waited in the tree for the king's men to leave before he sprung down to help me up. We got away with it, but only just. Since then we've agreed that he'll keep lookout on the ground. That way, if trouble is near, I'll already be safely hidden from view and he can quickly scramble up to join me. It's a much safer plan.

I take a couple of deep breaths and prepare for the next short climb. I sit up, deep in thought, planning a route and working out what I think I can manage. Suddenly, my concentration is broken. My jaw drops. I gasp and jump, wobbling nervously on the branch. I wasn't expecting to be interrupted here. I don't know whether to climb back down or to call out to Sekani. He's looking for danger but the danger is where we least expected it: here! My heart beats fast as I ponder what to do next. Two pairs of eyes are fixed on me, watching my every move. *Did they know we were here? Have they been watching us? Were they waiting for us to climb up, or were they hoping to stay hidden?* I can't tell. The faces of the boy and girl are giving away nothing. They continue to stare and I feel very uncomfortable. I don't look away though. I'm determined to be strong and I try to keep my face as expressionless as theirs. The girl's eyes are hard and dark. She seems tough. I watch the slightly older-looking boy instead. He's thinking. His eyes flicker as though he's just had an idea. I narrow mine, seeing an opportunity and hope that he'll be the first to break. I'm right.

"You're from Jericho, aren't you?" It's a demand rather than a question and I don't respond. I'm thinking fast. "You're a Canaanite." His friend looks annoyed that he's talking. She's glaring at him as though her look could stop him. I stay quiet, wondering what he really wants to know. And what she wants to hide. They are obviously not from Jericho and they are obviously up to something. I just don't know what. I want to know where Sekani is and whether he knows what's going on up here, but I daren't look away from the children. They may not know that he's there at all. I don't want to put my brother in any danger – I may need him to get me out of here. And I don't want to miss anything. I want to know what's going on. The boy tries again.

"You are, aren't you? You're from inside the wall."

"Gurion, be quiet," hisses the girl, looking really annoyed. "We don't know if we can trust—"

"She's from inside!" he whispers back. They're talking as though I'm not here at all. "Just think what she could tell us!"

What could I tell them? What do they want to know? Are they spies? Have they been sent to report on the city, ready for… No, of course not, Tabia. I laugh at myself. They're far too young. They're no older than I am. But what are they talking about?

"I just don't think we—"

"Daya, I know we need to get back. I understand what you told me, but this could be important too. She's from—"

"Then what's she doing out—"

"It doesn't matter. What's important is what I'll be able to—"

"And have you thought about what she'll be able to tell them?" The boy, Gurion, doesn't say anything else after this. I'm confused.

I watch the two of them glaring at each other and try to make sense of what I've heard. Daya obviously doesn't trust me and she's trying to stop Gurion saying too much. He wants to know something about Jericho. *But what? And why?* I am sure of one thing though. I'm convinced that the children are Israelites. Their names are foreign and they talked about needing to get back. *Where?* It occurs to me that the girl might actually be right. I might have something to learn from them as well. I wonder if they know where the men are that came to our house. *Do I trust them enough to ask?*

My thoughts are interrupted by a voice from below and I realise that I should've found a way to warn my brother sooner. It's too late now. I could kick myself.

"What's going on up there?" Sekani calls out. "Are you all right, Tabia? What can you see?"

The two strangers look at each other and grin. I do not. I may have just missed my chance to find out everything we need to know.

"She's fine," the boy shouts down in response. My cheeks and forehead burn hot with anger. "She's coming down now!"

16

"They ate some of the produce of the land."

Brilliant! The girl's eyes are darting around furiously. She's opened her mouth to speak, but she doesn't know what to say to me. I laugh at her as I swing down from my branch, which only makes her glare harder. I have an advantage now. She's annoyed. Daya always gives things away that she doesn't mean to when she's annoyed. That's why I tease her all the time. It's the best way to find out what's going on. Maybe this girl – *did he call her Tabia?* – will be the same.

I land lightly on the ground, face to face with the owner of the voice. He looks annoyed too, but there's a more determined look in his eyes. I draw my body up and lock my eyes onto his face. I can be determined too. Without looking away, or even blinking, I call out to Daya.

"What's going on? Where are you?"

"We're coming, Gurion, but she's a bit slow." I laugh. The boy pushes me aside and reaches out to support Tabia as she lowers herself down. I laugh again. Daya drops to the ground last and immediately turns her back on the strangers. She tiptoes to whisper in my ear. "Let's just go, Gu." I shake my head. My eyes are still fixed on the pair, who stay stubbornly silent.

"You're not going to get them to talk." I don't respond. I accept that it will be best to go back with Daya and join the Israelite men eventually, but there's no way I'm walking away from this opportunity. I am standing with two people who have more useful information than Jericho's walls have bricks and I'm not going back without it. I sidestep my sister and decide to try the friendly approach.

"So, is anyone else hungry?" Both girls glare at me, but the corners of the boy's mouth begin to turn upwards and his eyes soften a little.

"Actually, yes. I was thinking about breakfast," he admits. "Tabia…"

"I don't believe you, Sekani!"

"Please," he continues. His voice is kind but firm and I'm amazed when she responds. Tabia whispers something to Sekani on her way past that I don't manage to overhear. "It's all right, they're just…" but he thinks better of finishing the sentence.

"Daya, you should go too. You can help."

She folds her arms in protest and speaks almost under her breath. "I'm not going anywhere, Gurion. We don't know what—"

"But you like to cook," I insist, "and it's only fair that we share the workload." For a moment, she doesn't move and I think she's going to storm off in the direction of the camp without another word. I probably would have done if I were her. But she doesn't. Daya is a little more patient. She follows Tabia down a path between two fields, keeping a few paces behind and checking back over her shoulder often. *Why is she being so cautious?* I'm not sure what she thinks is going to happen.

"You are from Jericho, aren't you?" I begin, settling myself down on the ground and trying to seem casual. I'm desperate to know everything, but I don't want to appear too keen. I'm still trying to gain Sekani's trust. "What are you doing out here? And where is everyone else? It seems so quiet."

"Yes," he acknowledges. "It is." Then, after a pause. "I'm Sekani. You must be from Israel. Gurion, is it?"

I smile and nod, still trying to be friendly. Sekani seems reasonable, but he hasn't answered my questions. How hard can I push him? "You two seem to be looking for something," I prompt.

"And you two seem to be hiding from something! We weren't expecting to stumble across you in that tree. What are you doing here? Why aren't you with the rest of Israel? The army must be getting ready for the big battle. Why would you want to miss out on that?"

Wow! Apparently I'm not the only one with questions. Perhaps if I talk first, he'll be more willing to share what he knows, which actually seems to be a lot. It's worth a try. And I can't leave without finding out something useful. I mustn't. This is too good an opportunity. I'll do whatever it takes to get the information from this boy. That's what a good Israelite soldier would do.

"To be honest, it's not actually that exciting. The men are camping at Gilgal, waiting for their instructions and it's all a bit slow. That's why I'm out here..."

"At Gilgal? Then they've already crossed the river? All of them? How did they—?"

Why is he so interested? Suddenly, I'm afraid I've done the wrong thing by talking. So far, he hasn't told me anything useful at all and now Sekani knows exactly where Israel is camping. *Who is Sekani actually? Why is he here and what is he up to? This boy is clever.* My palms are sweaty. My plan was to make Israel see how useful I can be and I may just have proved the exact opposite. I'm scared and wondering how to fix this. I wipe my hands on my knees and try to listen. I mustn't show Sekani how nervous I am. I have to find a way to get him back to our camp so that he can't report back to Jericho's army – otherwise I'm in real trouble.

17

"A land flowing with milk and honey."

I check back over my shoulder one last time as Gurion and the Canaanite boy begin to blend in with the background. I can't help feeling that this is some sort of trap. We know absolutely nothing about these two and I'm not really comfortable with the situation I'm in. Gu didn't leave me much choice, but we should be sticking together. He'd never deliberately send me into danger, but he's too desperate for information to realise what's happening. *Where is she taking me?*

Between the tall stalks of barley, it's very difficult to tell where we're going. I know that we're moving closer to the city, but it's still a long way off. Even from within the crops, I can see its walls rising high into the air. They emerge out of the horizon like a rock face – but they're somehow even less welcoming. They seem to have been designed to warn people not to come too close. It's obvious straight away just how powerful Jericho really is. Everything around it seems to show it. The sun is glinting off golden fields across the vast plains for as far as I can see. Many fields have been harvested, so there are patches where the crops are shorter and flattened, but much of the land is still overgrown with the golden stems. The strong stalks have been abandoned by the farmers of Jericho and have now grown slightly wild, but their size and quality still shows just how talented and successful the farmers here are. Even the paths are clearly defined from being so well trodden. I feel small and insignificant in such a carefully planned environment and shabby compared to the wealth and power on display here. I think of Israel's army of all sorts and imagine the trained strength of Jericho's men and I shudder. *What are we doing here?*

I'm deliberately keeping my distance from Tabia, so I'll have time to run at the first sign of danger. Jericho is making me feel deeply uneasy. We're far from the city but its influence is everywhere. I feel trapped and find myself wishing for the natural wilderness we left behind. I force myself to stay alert; to concentrate on where Tabia is leading me and stay aware of my options for escaping. I don't trust this place and I don't trust her.

Tabia hasn't spoken to me at all so far. She hasn't even checked to see whether I'm following her but she knows I am. My footsteps are not loud, but there's nothing here to disguise the sound. It's eerily quiet. I think of the bustle of the camp as the morning manna is collected and promise myself I'll return there as soon as I can, with or without Gurion. This place is strange and unfriendly. Like the people. I question again what Tabia and Sekani are really doing out here.

Tabia turns off the path and into the field. She pushes the stalks of barley aside with an arm and wades straight in. For the first time, she turns to check that I'm following. She must notice the dubious look on my face, because she decides to speak.

"It's the quickest way to the food."

I'm confused, so I don't say anything, but I follow. It seems she might be getting breakfast after all. Still, I keep my distance, and I'm ready to run if necessary. Soon though, my curiosity starts to take over from my suspicion and I stride a little faster. We're approaching a clump of trees that stand out tall above the barley. They have shiny, narrow leaves and bright red flowers. I'm stunned. I've never seen a plant so pretty. As we approach, I find I can't look away. I'm intrigued by the bright red bursts standing out so beautifully against the glossy green of the tree. Tabia doesn't seem to notice. She's still focused on sweeping aside the barley to clear a path.

We reach the outcrop. I wander around the group of trees, taking in the image and forgetting to keep an eye on Tabia. Suddenly, she's right beside me and I jump.

"Hold these," she says, thrusting a handful of small, round, red objects into my hands and seeming not to notice my wide eyes. I stare at the pile, examining the objects, wondering what they are. Their skin is bright red with a yellowish base, and it looks tough. A wobbly crown sticks out of each imperfect sphere. As I lift my hands to get a closer look they roll slightly, feeling rough against my palms.

"What are they?" I ask, looking up for the first time to see Tabia plucking more of them from the tree. She taps each one lightly, before twisting it gently from the branch. It dawns on me that this is what we're supposed to eat. I sniff doubtfully at the pile.

"Pomegranates," she says. "Haven't you seen one before?"

I shake my head. My stomach churns at the thought of putting these things anywhere near my mouth.

18

"I have given Jericho into your hand."

"I'd love to," I say, hoping I don't sound too enthusiastic. I'm still trying to be a little bit cautious around Gurion and Daya because we don't really know them yet, but the doubts I had about them are fading fast. Gurion is actually really friendly and talkative. I thought he was rude to begin with - he laughed at Tabia - but I think he must have been nervous or something. He's just offered to take us back to the Israelite camp so that we can see what's going on there for ourselves. He doesn't seem to mind that I had so many questions and once the girls had gone he was much easier to talk to. Maybe he didn't know whether he could trust us either. I still don't think Daya is convinced she can. And Tabia's unusually quiet too. Girls can be funny like that though.

"I'm surprised Israel hasn't attacked sooner," I say, throwing an empty fruit skin over my shoulder and reaching for another swollen pomegranate, "considering the battle is already won". Gurion looks up. His cheeks are full and juice dribbles down his chin. He wipes it with the back of his hand, but he's still chewing too much to speak, so I carry on. "Ever since those men came, the whole of Jericho has been in a panic. They're totally petrified because they know what your people have already done. They know they can't do anything to stop you, so they're just waiting. It's a bit pathetic really." Gurion hasn't looked away from me since I started speaking. He gulps the last of his pomegranate down and turns to Daya, who only raises her eyebrows. His eyes dart around as though he's searching for words. "I assume that the men did report back? We didn't see them pass, but if Israel's already at Gilgal... How did you all cross that river, by the way?" I'm deliberately leading him for the information I need. After breakfast we're going to join Israel just like I planned back in Jericho and I'm itching to get going. I wait for Gurion to give me the crucial information about the spies. Our first job is to track them down and confront them about their promise. Today's going really well. We've made a breakthrough. Once we know our family are safe, we can relax and enjoy the sight of those hateful king's men cowering under someone else's command for a change. I can't wait!

"What do you mean, 'the battle's already won'?" asks Gurion, starting hungrily on another pomegranate and taking me right back to the beginning. "Jericho's army is so strong. They're hardly going to stand back and watch us take the city. They must be planning some sort of defence... and then there are those incredible walls."

"But I think that's the only plan they do have - the walls. They are genuinely scared of you..."

"You're serious aren't you?" Gurion stops eating and leans forward with real interest in what I'm saying. It seems this information is totally new to him and he's finding it hard to accept. "You're saying that a city the size and strength of Jericho is actually scared of a nation of tent-dwellers with no obvious battle strategy?"

I sigh, and start again with the basics. I just want to get moving now, but I also need to keep Gurion on my side. "Israel is a scary thought for Jericho *because* it's such an unusual opponent. If it were just another army, Jericho would know exactly what to do – they'd win the fight in their sleep – but you... you're different. Israel crosses huge rivers and survives for years without food and..." I hesitate. "... and everyone's saying your God has given you the city. How can Jericho possibly fight that? Of course they're scared!"

A strange look crosses Gurion's face. He lets his unfinished fruit fall to the ground. I frown instinctively. There's a glint in his eye that makes me uncomfortable. Suddenly the friend I've been chatting to all morning has gone and the nasty predator we first met has returned. *Have I misjudged this boy?* Perhaps I trusted him too much. I look to Tabia for reassurance, but she looks worried too. For a few seconds, everyone is lost in thought. Nobody says anything and I frantically review my options. *Will they still take us to Gilgal?* If I can talk to the spies, everything will be fine. I look again at Gurion and have a horrible feeling that I've given away something I shouldn't have. *What though?* He's got the satisfied look of someone who's just found what they were looking for. *But what did I say*? I wish I knew what he was thinking. The horrible silence drags on. I wipe the sweat from my forehead.

"So you're running away?" The voice belongs to Daya, who hasn't spoken a word until now.

"Running away?"

"You seem very sure that Israel will conquer Jericho. I suppose you wanted to get out while you still had chance. Where will you go? What will you do now?"

Running away? Do we really seem like the cowardly type? I'm temporarily confused. *Can Daya really have misjudged us so badly?* I'm offended that she would think... But perhaps I'm not the only one finding it hard to know what's going on.

"Or will you report back everything that Gurion's told you? Will you try to give Jericho an advantage against us?" She sounds bitter, but I suspect that's exactly what Gurion's planning to do with the information I've just shared.

I smile weakly, unsure how to explain. I stammer clumsily until Tabia steps in to help me. She speaks very calmly.

"Actually, we're not running away," she states very simply. "Our family is not very popular with Jericho's army. If you live where we do, you're not considered to be worth very much. They can be extremely cruel. So we don't really respect the king's men - you heard my brother call them pathetic. That's actually quite polite considering how we feel about them. But my aunt was almost caught talking to your spies - she was helping them and they've promised to protect us all during the attack - and now—"

"Now we want to join Israel," I finish for her. "We believe your God is going to destroy Jericho. We want to make sure our family aren't destroyed too... because not everyone in

Jericho is like those soldiers. Thanks to your spies, we're on very dangerous territory in our own home."

"And because a promise was made," Tabia adds.

"Your lives will be spared, because you protected the lives of the spies," says Daya. "Our father told us the story, but–"

"You knew about this? Will you help us get our family out then?"

"I... I did, but I didn't realise it was you. I... I'd like to help." Daya looks almost sorry for me. "But you can't just walk into Gilgal! What made you think that–" I look from her to Gurion, who shuffles uncomfortably. "Gurion, these are Canaanites! If we were seen with–" She stops without finishing, but I get the idea.

"We were promised protection from your army," I protest. I'm getting frustrated with so much talking. I push myself to my feet, dropping my half-eaten pomegranate. I don't really understand what the problem is and I want answers from these men. "You know the story; others must know who we are too. We need to find–"

"I'm really sorry. I didn't trust you when we first saw you. I thought you were..." She shakes her head. "Now, I do understand why you're out here, but... They won't be expecting to see you here. You're supposed to be–"

"Where?" I retaliate, my voice rising in annoyance. "Inside the walls, waiting patiently for you to come and destroy the city?" Tabia stands up slowly and puts a hand gently on my arm to calm me down. I shrug it off.

"Exactly," replies Daya calmly. I shake my head and walk away before I explode.

19

"All who are with her in the house shall live."

"I am really sorry," I say again, to Tabia this time. She's about to run after her brother but she hesitates.

"Thanks, but that doesn't change… I need to find—"

"Wait!" I say. I'm begging. I really want the chance to explain if she'll let me. I can't take the Canaanites to Gilgal, but I want them to understand why not. When Dad told us their story around the fire, it was just another story. I listened sleepily and imagined characters in a make-believe land and thought it was all a great adventure. Now it's totally different. Now I've met Tabia and Sekani and they're real people. People with emotions who make mistakes and have hopes and plans and… tempers. They remind me of myself. And Gurion. He came out here in search of adventure. These children are mixed up in one and heading for disaster. I can't let them carry on. I can't let Tabia go after Sekani without telling her what I know. It wouldn't be right.

"Tabia," I begin again. "I really thought you were looking for information to report to Jericho's army. That's why I didn't speak to you for so long. If I'd known… Well, I'm sorry." Tabia is looking down the path where Sekani stormed off. I can see she's desperate to get to him and she's only half-listening. I need to win her attention. "I wouldn't have blamed you. It's what Gurion is planning to do." She turns her head. "I'm only here to get him back. He needs to be at the camp, but he's so keen to find an adventure and make himself a hero that he'd do anything… including, it seems, lead you two into danger."

"It's a bit late to be sorry, Daya." Tabia has folded her arms across herself and is shaking her head in disbelief. "Sekani's already in danger. You haven't helped us at all. I have to go before he…" She trails off and takes a few quick steps before turning back to add, "The king's men would never ask us to help them. They're far too important to rely on our kind of 'scum'. If they did ask, we'd never do it. I wouldn't help those beasts if they were the last… And I don't know why you're so concerned about your brother. He seems quite capable of looking after himself. He won't listen to you, or anyone else. If he lived in Jericho, he'd make a great soldier – they only care about looking good too."

Gurion is leaning back against the tree, watching the exchange with an amused expression. He only smirks about what Tabia thinks of him, still not caring at all what will happen to her and her brother. Still, I assume, planning to use their information to gain status with Israel's officers, whatever the cost to anyone else.

"You're absolutely right," I reply, wiping the smile off Gu's face. He scowls at me. "He's being stubborn and cruel, and if it was anyone else, I'd leave them to find out how pathetic and lonely that makes them. But he's my brother. You'd do anything for Sekani, and I'm no different." Tabia's face softens a little. Something I'm saying must make sense to her. "I'm not leaving Gurion until I've talked sense into him and convinced him to come back to Gilgal. His biggest fault was not having all the facts about what's going on there which is exactly the same mistake you two are making. He left to make something happen because he didn't understand that it was already happening."

"Fine. Gurion made a mistake. That doesn't help me. You're still going back to join Israel and attack Jericho. My family are still inside those walls and, whether you decide to tell your soldiers what Sekani told you or not, Israel is going to win. It makes no difference. The city is yours. All I want to do is stop my brother from making himself an easy first target and get my family out before it's too late." I'm stunned. I don't know what to say. The way Tabia explains the situation, I understand why she's so angry. I'd be mad too. "The only useful thing I've learned from you is that your spies lied – they promised to help us and now you tell us we're as good as dead if we even set foot near your camp. We're not safe, they won't protect us, and we're totally on our own. If you can't be any more help than that, then I have to—"

"You have to get back inside those walls with your family."

"No. I don't, Daya," she's almost shouting now. "I have to get them out. I really can't believe my aunt trusted those men – and I can't believe Sekani trusted you – she got your spies out of Jericho alive because she believes in your God but apparently nobody in the whole of Israel will do the same for her. Jericho's people are right to be afraid of you – you're all totally heartless."

Sekani reappears – presumably he's heard everything – and takes Tabia by the hand. She's shaking. Perhaps it's anger, maybe fear of what she thinks is going to happen, but I don't have time to work out which; I take my opportunity while she's quiet. "When my father told us how a woman had helped Israel's men to escape, he said that her family would be protected in return. My father is a good man and an officer. I believe him." Sekani is holding Tabia to comfort her. He seems to be listening to me. I can't tell whether or not Tabia is too. "He said that all who were inside her house would live. That's why you need to go back. That's why the army won't be expecting to see you out here." Sekani wipes a tear from Tabia's cheek and she looks up.

"Why should I believe you?" she asks. Apparently she was listening. Her voice is calmer again, but still strong. I think Tabia would like to trust what I'm saying; she just can't allow herself to believe that I'm being honest. I'm aware that the lives of Tabia, Sekani and their whole family may depend on what I choose to say next. I close my eyes and think extremely carefully before asking a question of my own.

"After the spies left, did you see a piece of red cord tied in any of your windows?"

20

"Jericho was tightly shut."

"Sekani! The window! I saw it, but I didn't… Red; bright red! A signal! It makes perfect sense now. A sign to show them… But I nearly took it down. I thought… I could've killed them all. Sekani, this means…! Sekani?"

"Slow down, Tabia. I don't know what you're talking about."

"The red cord in the window. When we left. I saw it there and I thought… but that doesn't matter now. This means she's telling the truth, Sekani! It means the spies were telling the truth too. It means—"

"Tabia, I didn't see a red cord. Are you sure it was there? You're not just—"

"Yes! I remember! I remember wondering what it was doing there and thinking it was dangerous because it drew too much attention to the house and then not being able to go back up to move it because you were already—"

"You're sure?"

"Yes, Sekani! Yes! I'm absolutely sure. We're safe! We're going to survive after all!" I throw my arms around my brother's neck and jump up and down for joy. The relief floods through my body and I relax for the first time in days. I feel light and warm and… I must've been so worried and tense all this time – I hadn't even realised. Tears are escaping from my eyes now and I pull away from my brother slightly to wipe them from my lashes; I don't want to look babyish. As I do, I notice his expression. Even through the wet blur it's obvious that Sekani isn't smiling. *Why not? This is great news. What's wrong?* He can't have understood what I've been saying.

"Sekani, we're safe! It's all going to be OK…"

"No, Tabia. If there really was a red cord in the window…" I open my mouth to protest, but Sekani cuts me off. "…and I do believe you saw it there – it means that Daya's telling us the truth."

"Yes, I know. That's what—"

"And that means the rest of what she's been saying is right as well. Tabia, we should be inside the walls… inside the house. At this exact moment." My chest tightens. I feel like I've been punched. "The cord is a sign of the promise, but it only protects those in the household it marks out. The others are safe now, but—"

"But we're not." I finish for him. I flop to the ground, unable to keep standing on my wobbly legs. My body feels heavy and limp as though it doesn't even belong to me and my brain is refusing to work at all. Sekani sits beside me. Neither of us speaks. I don't think there's anything to say that would take away this sickening realisation.

"Well," says Gurion, getting to his feet and breaking the tension. "It was nice to have met you. I'm glad Daya could help. We need to get back to our camp now. Perhaps we'll see you when—"

"Gurion!" Daya snaps. I watch the two of them begin to bicker but it's all happening in slow motion and their words aren't reaching my brain – it still seems stuck on one thought. We were wrong. We were determined to help, but we got everything so badly wrong.

"I'm going, Daya. Stay if you want to. I have vital information to give—"

"Surely you don't still think that's important?"

"Jericho's army are scared of us. They have no plan. Of course it's important for Israel's men to know that. And I'm the only one who can—"

"Oh, go then." Daya sighs, shaking her head.

"Wait, Gurion! We're coming!" Sekani has leapt to his feet and grabbed Gurion's arm. "Come on, Tabia! Let's go! Move!"

"No, Sekani! Tabia was right. It doesn't make any difference what Gurion tells them. Israel has won the battle already. You need to go home. You can't come anywhere near Gilgal. It's not safe!" Daya's eyes are wide with disbelief and fear. I'm so confused and dazed, I don't understand what anybody's talking about any more, but Daya's expression at this moment fixes itself in my mind. I suddenly grasp her genuine concern for us. "Go home, Sekani! Take Tabia and go. Don't worry about—"

"The gate is closed." Sekani is matter of fact. His voice and face are inexpressive, but I know his heart must be in pieces. "There's been no sign of anyone from Jericho for days. We can't go home. There's no way in."

"Sekani?" My voice comes out weak and wobbly. "What will we do?" I'm fighting back tears.

"We're going to find the men that made the promise. They'll have to help us get back in, or keep us safe until they get the others out." He sounds determined. "They know us, Tabia. They'll sort this out." Daya spins him round and looks him straight in the eye.

"No, Sekani! You can't ! That's madness. It's not safe!"

"It will be if Gurion takes us. He wants to tell Israel's army what's happening in Jericho. Let him! He can tell everyone who we are at the same time and..."

"Oh, no. I'm going back, but I'm not taking you! I can't be seen with you. We shouldn't even have spoken to you at all. You're putting me in danger."

"We're putting you...?" Sekani's sentence trails off in total disbelief.

"Gurion." Daya is tackling her brother now. "You wanted an adventure. You wanted to make a difference – an important difference. This is it! It can't get any more important. These people *are* the story of Jericho that the whole of Israel will be telling for years to come. They are the reason our men are able to fight and win. Without them it wouldn't be happening at all. You have an opportunity to help them – to make a difference to *the* story – and you're running away! What a hero." The last words are full of sisterly scorn, and it works. For the first time, Gurion does look ashamed of his selfish behaviour.

"I just want to be a good soldier," he mutters.

"Then fight the right battle," says Daya. Her voice is softer now and there's a kind look in her eyes. She doesn't say any more, but leaves him to think about what that means.

In the quiet that settles, I think about why we left Jericho in the first place. What was it that made us so certain it was the right thing to do? How did we get it so wrong? What did we miss? I look at Sekani and the uncomfortable thought occurs to me that it was all his idea. I hadn't wanted to go. We're in this disaster because I listened to Sekani. I feel disappointed in him, in myself and more unhappy than ever. Fortunately, I don't have time to dwell on the feeling for long before Gurion speaks again and the situation begins to improve. Drastically.

"If the main gate is closed, how did you two ever get out of there in the first place?" He's only thinking aloud, but I could hug him.

"Sekani, the rope!"

21

"They marched around the city once..."

Between the campground at Gilgal and the commanding walled city of Jericho the nation of Israel was under way. At the front of the procession were the armed men: the newly commissioned young warriors, eager for action and full of pride. They marched in step, setting the pace for all who followed behind with the rhythm of their feet, but their voices were silent. Not a single word crossed the lips of any of the men.

The distinctive call of seven rams' horns resounded across the barley fields early that morning. Seven priests marched behind the armed men, sounding the battle cry continuously from the instruments as they progressed towards the city. They walked just ahead of the golden ark, calling attention to the visible signal of God's presence among his people.

Behind the ark came the rear guard. While the armed men of Israel signalled its arrival to the Canaanites, those who followed reinforced its importance and value by their protecting presence. They were there to emphasise the central, guiding authority of their God and his promises to them. The Israelites introduced the ark as the Canaanites would present a Pharoah, marking it out as special, significant and set apart. Still no one spoke in the entire nation of Israel. No one announced their arrival. No one shouted a battle cry; or orders for the men; or even a challenge to the army of Jericho. Israel's people simply, and silently, marched.

As the sun rose, glinting on the tips of the wheat and barley in the fields, the Israelites made their way from Gilgal to Jericho. They moved in formation through the fields, grateful for the small patches of shade as they passed beneath the occasional sycamore fig. Soon, the secured city gates came into view. The huge structures rose impressively out of the hill, towering high above the people of Israel, both welcoming guests to the rich and powerful city and shutting out unwanted visitors. This might have hindered an enemy who planned to gain entry, but God had given the Israelite army a unique plan.

Before the armed men reached the base of the hill on which Jericho stood, they turned and continued to march on flat ground, following the perimeter of the city wall. As they did so, faces began to appear at the windows and on the roofs, attracted by the sound of the rams' horns and fascinated by the sight of the Israelite procession. Jericho's citizens had known that this was coming. They had anticipated the moment with dread, having shared stories of Israel's past conquests. Word had spread quickly through the streets that Israel had arrived and the collective curiosity of a nation had brought its inhabitants to the outer wall in their masses. That curiosity was being encouraged now by the odd behaviour of the outsiders. Not only had they failed to attack, choosing instead to parade around the perimeter of the city wall, but they were doing it in total silence. This was too much for the gossiping tongues of

Jericho to resist. The walls were alive with whispering speculation and scornful abuse. Fingers pointed, heads shook in disbelief, laughter rang out and eyebrows were raised. Yet behind the bravado ran a current of concern. The unexpected behaviour of Israel had unsettled the people of Jericho. They had not predicted such a strange tactic and were immediately suspicious. Where was the twist? What were these men planning? Beneath the mask of mockery was an expression of bewilderment that betrayed itself in the sideways glances between family members, the angry protests about the lack of response from the king's men and the painstaking attention everyone was paying to the Israelites' every step.

But at one window high in the wall to the north of the city, a face looked away into the distance – beyond the procession; not occupied with absorbing the detail of the bizarre battle approach, but scouring the horizon instead in search of something more significant. Everyone else's attention was on the seven men blowing rams' horns and leading an ornate golden box, but this woman focused intently on the fields in the distance, longing for the smallest sign of hope. While other faces showed intrigue, awe and trepidation, hers showed only sorrow. Her hand clasped a small segment of scarlet cord and a tear trickled silently down her face.

Concealed from her view, high in the branches of a sycamore fig in the middle of the barley fields, four children looked on in stunned silence, each lost in their own interpretation of what this procession meant for them – and wondering what they could do about it.

22

"… and returned to the camp."

Wow! I'm stunned into silence. The four of us are clinging to various branches of this fig tree, staring into the distance. None of us has spoken a syllable for ages and nobody seems to want to be the first to move either. I'm actually numb from standing in the same position for so long with my foot wedged between the tree trunk and another large bough. I'm afraid if I do try to move, my legs will give way and I'll fall. But I'm squashed and uncomfortable – and confused. I'm gaping out between a couple of densely covered branches, hanging on for support, and wondering what has just happened. For the first time since Daya and I met the Canaanites, we all seem to be agreeing – or perhaps it would be more accurate to say that we're all just numb with shock.

Personally, I'm still getting over the jolt of seeing Israel march right up to Jericho's gate. I thought that was going to be it! I thought they were going to attack and that I was going to miss out on all the action and… and I actually just wanted to yell out to them to wait for me. What surprised me the most is how devastated I felt not to be there. I'd have given anything just to march alongside the other men: nothing special, no commanding position or privileged information or superior status, just Gurion, there, in the midst of it all. I came here searching for a way to mark myself out, but seeing them there together and united, I realised how much I miss being around others. I didn't want to be the one watching from the sidelines any more, having my own adventure. I wanted to belong again. And I don't think I'm the only one.

I look again at the pale faces of Sekani and Tabia. They still haven't spoken, but I can guess what they are feeling and I have to admit that I actually feel sorry for them. They risked everything to come out here and help their family and now they're almost certainly too late to help themselves. It makes me ashamed. All my efforts were for myself – I wanted to be noticed. The two figures I am watching now didn't think of themselves at all. Even now, Sekani has an arm protectively around his sister, who is shaking a little although it's nowhere near late enough to be cold yet. The rope they were relying on to get back inside the wall had gone by the time we arrived – I suspect it had gone long before that – and after today, security in Jericho is likely to be tighter than ever. When Israel's army approached the city, the two of them watched wide-eyed. We all thought that was the end. I can only imagine how they felt – that it was all over: that they were too late. Tabia had tears streaming down her cheeks, but wouldn't look away. Sekani's expression was blank, his eyes were empty, but he must have been confused and angry too. And then the attack didn't come and Israel went back past us to Gilgal and none of us really understand what happened or why. *Do they feel any relief, or is it worse now, wondering what's coming next?* I think of my own family. I think of what I'd do in Sekani's situation. My heart actually aches to think about it: I feel sick. I question how I'd feel if I knew I couldn't ever see my mother and father again. I don't want to think about that. I can't. Something inside me finally snaps. My mind literally switches off and all I know is that I have to move. I have to act. I have to go home.

"Daya, let's go!"

She turns her head slowly around and finally tears her uneasy eyes away from our friends. "Gurion?"

"We need to go. We have to get back. Find out what's going on. We—"

"Gurion," she whispers, though neither Sekani or Tabia appear to be listening to us. They're still gazing sadly at the city walls. "We can't just go and leave—"

"What about your duty to Israel?" I'm teasing her. I've reverted to what I know best to try to shift the tense, uncomfortable atmosphere here. My voice is falsely confident. Still, it wobbles. I can't pretend that life is normal now. Things have changed – I've changed – and anyway Daya sees straight through my bravado. I look at my feet. I feel strangely out of place in my own skin. I don't know how to be anything other than confrontational with Daya – it's been that way for so long.

"We can't leave them, Gurion."

"We have to, Daya." It's a huge effort to speak honestly to my sister about my thoughts, but it's the only way to put things right now. "I was wrong. I've behaved terribly. I need to go back and apologise to Father."

"But that's not going to—"

"Help?" I finish for her. "It may be the only thing that will. There's nothing we can do for Sekani and Tabia here. I need to find out from Father what is going on. I need to explain what's happened and ask his advice, and I need to..."

"You're going to ask advice from Dad?" She is clearly stunned. I carry on without commenting. This is important.

"... ask to be circumcised like the rest of the men: to show God that I trust his plan and that I will follow it; that I don't care if I'm leading armies with Joshua or carrying equipment with the donkeys. I want to be part of the story, Daya. I need to be in the right place now."

Daya blinks but doesn't respond straight away. She is clearly torn about what to say next. Her forehead is crinkled and her eyes narrowed in difficult thought. I need her to believe this is the right thing for us to do. After a painfully long silence, I can't wait any more. I really need to act quickly on what I've said – what I believe. I interrupt her thoughts.

"Daya, you've said all along that our place is in the camp. That people should be able to rely on us to know that simple things will be done. That it all helps in the—"

"I know." She's holding back tears of frustration. "I should have been there. I've let them down. I promised to help with... But it'd be wrong to walk away from this too. We can't just leave... They're going to... I don't know what to do, Gu. I don't know!"

"That's why we need Dad's advice." I hope I sound calmer than I feel. "We're not the only ones in the wrong place now and we will do all we can to help Sekani and Tabia – I promise – but they can't come with us. It's not safe. I'm ashamed that I ever suggested that. And we can't stay here and base our choices on guesswork and theories either. We need to find out as much as we can so that we can make a plan to get all four of us back where we belong."

I can see Daya is still reluctant to leave the others but there's nothing more I can say to convince her. She has to make her own decision now. I have to do what I believe is best for all of us.

"Sekani," I say, putting a hand gently on his shoulder. "I'll be back as soon as I can. Stay out of sight and look after Tabia. I'll do everything I can to..." Sekani doesn't speak, but his eyes meet mine for the first time since the procession and he nods. I smile with relief. He understands. I swing my legs over the branch and scramble down the tree trunk as fast as I dare.

PART FOUR: THE SCARLET CORD

"Be strong and courageous."

23

"They rose early at the dawning of the day."

I'm wide awake, tossing and turning under my blanket. It's still really dark inside the tent. And outside too. I know I should be trying to get more sleep, and I am, but there's lots to think about. I can't stop going over today's task again and again in my mind. I have to be sure I've thought of everything; planned for everything; missed nothing. This is it now. My one final chance to put everything right and it absolutely has to work. There's no room for making mistakes. No time to hang around now. I'm going through the day, step by step, making sure I'm clear about where Israel will be, and when. Making sure I know where it's safe for me to be. Making sure I haven't forgotten anything vitally important. I don't think I have – I can't think of anything else.

There's no sign of movement in the campground yet. It must still be very early in the morning. I should rest. I flip over onto my other side and close my eyes tightly again. But I'm not asleep. I'm still thinking about the day ahead of me with a mixture of excitement and dread.

Sunrise: Israel will move quickly into formation. They'll set out as soon as possible. Gurion will be at the front with the armed men. I'll be following a safe distance behind the rear guard.

At the sycamore fig, I'll slip into the wheat field to hide. When I'm totally sure the parade has moved on enough so no one will notice me climbing, I'll climb into the tree. This should be the *easy* part. How hard can it be to simply fade away into the shadows, and to blend back into the crowd when Israel return to Gilgal? Then if Sekani and Tabia are there, I'll tell them *everything* I know and we'll make our plan.

During the march: this is where things are going to get a lot more complicated. Every day so far this week, Israel have marched once around Jericho's city walls and returned straight to Gilgal. I know roughly how long it takes them to travel from Gilgal to Jericho, circle the city and march back. Today though, Israel plan to march seven times around the city wall – one of the useful things Gu found out from Dad. But will they keep to the same pace they've used so far, slow down as they get tired or speed up with excitement? It's impossible to predict. And what will happen after the seventh time? Will Israel return to Gilgal? I don't know. Today is going to involve much more guesswork than I'd like. I'll have to be more alert, more aware – and more adaptable. I can't plan properly for this part and that concerns me. That's what's keeping me awake now.

There's going to be a lot to do in the short time we have too, however long that turns out to be. I'm praying that Sekani and Tabia will be waiting for me today. They need to know what I know. I have to talk to them. They need to understand how urgent today's task is. When I've broken the difficult news to them, we'll have to speed down from the tree undetected and edge closer to the city walls. Today we have to get them back inside the walls – back inside their home: back inside the promise of protection – and do it all before it's too late; before the battle begins!

It's good to be prepared for potential problems. So: we'll need to be constantly aware of Israel's location. We'll need to make contact with Sekani and Tabia's family on the inside – though chances are they've already arranged that. That's probably what they were doing this week while I was in the camp. We'll need to time the rope drop and the wall climb precisely so it isn't spotted by any (not a single one!) of the many citizens of Jericho who'll be lining the walls to watch the proceedings like they have every day so far this week. I cringe. That's a lot to keep in mind. That's a lot that could go wrong. Still, I'm trying to feel confident. Gurion's input has been great. Between the other three of us we should be able to cope. We should be able to succeed against the two great nations of Israel and Jericho. We should.

I'm a bit nervous that Gurion won't be there to help us, but there's nothing I can do about that. He sacrificed his own involvement in this adventure to get the information we needed to make our plan. If he hadn't been to Dad for forgiveness, I wouldn't know what I do now about Israel's plans. We wouldn't know where to begin. He put Sekani and Tabia's needs before himself. He swallowed his pride and went to Dad. I'm proud of Gu. It took a lot for him to step back and do that. It's possibly the most heroic thing he's ever done.

Gurion wanted to be more involved, but he also realised it was important to be in the right place – he said if God had a plan it was probably going to be a better one than anything he could come up with. That's quite a big admission for Gu. Dad agreed to circumcise him even though Gu had missed out on the big event because he'd come back and said sorry, and because "If you're going to march with the other armed men leading our nation, you need to be prepared before God, Gurion". This was the closest Dad was going to get to saying that Gu's a man now and Gu knew it. He grew taller with pride and he's been much less hot-headed ever since.

What he didn't account for though was spending the rest of the week in the tent recovering. I don't think he had much fun, but he swallowed his pride and got on with it. He even started being a bit more caring too, which is nice but weird. He listened to my worries each evening. Without interrupting! And he gave me good advice. He'll make a great officer one day.

Ever since I'd realised the trouble Sekani and Tabia were in, I'd wanted to help them, but being back in the campground again, life got back to normal and I nearly forgot. While Dad and Gu were busy with their man time, I did what I know best – helping Mum with the jobs. It came so naturally and felt so right to be serving Israel in the preparation phase that I nearly forgot about the others altogether. It was only when Gu asked me how they were getting on that I felt a stab of guilt. He reminded me that they wanted to put mistakes right too – and we should help them do that if we possibly could. He's right and I still feel guilty that I put them behind me so easily. Helping them doesn't have to mean letting my parents down. I've done everything I can to help prepare things here and today I'm going to give all my time and energy to help my friends.

"Daya!" It's Gu. He's shaking me gently. "Daya, wake up!" I'd drifted off to sleep again, thinking about the day. I open my eyes to the first rays of sun entering my tent. This is it. No more thinking. No more planning. It's time to go. "Daya, come on! It's time to go!"

24

"They marched..."

I've already been awake and watching the horizon for a while when Israel's first row of armed men finally comes into view. I've been straining my eyes for signs of movement in the semi-darkness and I find it hard to focus on the shape for long. I look at Sekani who's lost in his own thoughts, then back to the distant shadow. *Please God, if you exist, bring Daya and Gurion back today.* It's slightly clearer now and growing larger with every second that passes. The army will be here soon. I'm worried. How long can this siege go on? We have to do something soon. So far, nothing seems to have worked. We need help. I close my eyes tightly and concentrate. *Rahab believes you can make odd things happen. Impossible things. Well, I'm in an impossible situation. I need your help. Help me. Help us. Me and Sekani. Send Gurion and Daya. Or send those men. Send anyone who can fix this mess. Please. Please get us back home where we'll be safe again. I can't do this on my own.*

When I open my eyes again, Israel is already passing beneath my branch and I spot Daya, crouching in the corn not far away. I nod my head with relief. *Thank you.* I'm so pleased to see Daya. But I'm still nervous. She's on her own. *Where's Gurion? What's happened? Something's wrong*. As Daya scrambles silently up the sycamore trunk, Israel is moving steadily away towards Jericho. I have to bite my lip to stop myself calling out and drawing attention to her, the tree or, worst of all, to Sekani and me: inhabitants of Jericho – so by definition enemies of Israel – outside of the wall!

"Daya, where have you been?" I whisper, as soon as she's close enough to hear. "Where's Gurion? What's going on? You said you'd come back. We've been—"

"Hang on," she says, stretching an arm up. "Let me just…" I grab her wrist and hold tightly. Sekani reaches down and gives her a tug.

"We waited for you! Gurion told us to wait, so we did and… Where is Gurion? We waited for ages and then…" I know I'm babbling. I'm worried – I don't know what we're going to do – and I'm angry about the last few days.

"Are you all right?" Sekani asks. Daya nods and smiles. "I'm glad you're here. We were worried about you. Is Gurion safe?"

"Yes."

"Is he coming?"

"No. He wanted to, but he can't. He's… He found out something from Dad. I have to talk to you."

"He promised," I protest. "He told us to wait and—"

"I know." Daya seems tense too. "Please, let me—"

"It's been five days! We haven't seen you at all. We thought you weren't—"

"I came back!" she snaps.

"When?"

"The third day that Israel marched. And yesterday as well!"

"Really?"

"Yes. The first day after we left you – the second day of marching – Gu had to talk with our dad. There was a lot to explain and then they had to…" she shifts her eyes uncomfortably and lowers her voice "… do the operation." I don't say anything. I fold my arms across my chest. I don't know what she's talking about. "It's something they've done to all the men who are marching… because they're God's people." I'm still not sure what Daya means. "Anyway, that happened and I did some jobs in the camp."

"And meanwhile we didn't know what was going on, or where you were or what to do!"

"But I came back the next day – as soon as I could! Gurion couldn't, because – well, he wanted to, but he had to rest and recover this week – so he sent me alone. But when I got up here, you'd disappeared. I didn't know where you'd gone… or whether you were coming back. I thought maybe I was too late."

"So you just left?"

"Yes! What else was I supposed—"

"Arguing about that isn't going to help us now." It's Sekani. "What's going on, Daya? Where's Gurion?"

"With the other men. He's marching with them today."

Then nobody says anything for a while. Sekani stares back towards the city. *Is that where Gurion's been all week? Every day when the army marched around the city, was he there with them? Has he forgotten that he'd promised to come back or was that a lie?* Thinking about it makes me mad. I can't stand the silence.

"I told you we should wait longer, Sekani." He's still staring into the distance. "Daya came and we weren't here." He ignores me. "Sekani, if you hadn't made us…"

"Tabia, she's here now. It doesn't matter." His calm voice is making me feel even angrier. I want to go home. I don't want to die here. We haven't even come close to the wall in five days and I don't understand anything that's happening. Israel just keep marching around. Why would they do that? I don't understand. My brother doesn't seem to share my concerns. He's chatting with Daya now. "How far do you think they've got?" he asks her.

"I don't know. It's hard to say."

"I want to show you something. When you came, we were in the field. We were trying to get someone in the house to see us. I thought we should be doing something, not just sitting here waiting. But the king's men were out, wandering around outside the walls. Not marching, not patrolling, just looking around. It was odd. They've done it every day as far as I can work out. When Israel has gone back, I'll take you. You can see what I'm talking about."

"Sekani, they won't be there today."

"I'm sure they will. It's the same every day. After Israel march, the king's men—"

"Today's different. That's why Gu is with the men now. That's what he found out..." I sigh loudly. I've heard enough. This chat isn't getting us anywhere.

What does she mean "Today is different"? I'm sure Daya knows much more than she's told us so far. But I don't see anything different. The army is marching, just the same as they have for the past six days. I suppose they can't keep on forever, but they haven't stopped yet. Maybe they'll carry on until Jericho's army respond in some way.

"So, did you?" asks Daya, interrupting my thoughts.

"Did I what?"

"Get someone in the house to see you." I shake my head. "Oh."

"I know. We were upset that we couldn't get any closer. It's getting frustrating. The next day we tried a different approach and we came to Gilgal after the army had set out. We thought we might find you or Gurion. But there were still far too many people in the camp. We didn't know where you'd be and we knew it wasn't safe to come too close, even with the men away. We couldn't see any sign of you, so we–"

"I couldn't get away. Mum was cross that I'd disappeared the day before and tired from doing my work as well as her own so she gave me our neighbours' children to look after for the day."

"We came back when the men returned and tried the wall again."

"I couldn't get away. I couldn't leave them alone and there's no way I could have brought them here."

"The soldiers were out, gazing around again. Looking blankly at the ground and the edges of the field. I don't know what they—"

"Mum kept me busy with jobs all the next day too. They were probably trying to work out what the Israelites had done."

"What they'd done?"

"They'll be confused. They probably don't understand why Israel haven't attacked, so they'll assume it's a trick. They'll be looking for signs of damage, or preparation - anything really to explain the weird behaviour."

"They're not the only ones who are confused."

"They won't find anything. Israel's men are only marching. They're not using that as a cover for anything."

"So what...?" I begin.

"Following instructions. I don't know any more than that."

"But you said it's different." I say it like a question. I hope she'll explain. "You said today is different." Daya still doesn't respond. I ask her outright. "What's different, Daya? What did you find out?" There's a long silence. I watch Daya. Tabia watches her too. She has something to say. I realise I'm holding my breath.

"This is it." She says quietly. "It's all going to end today. I don't know how exactly, but..." Tabia lets out a distressed cry.

"... today is your last chance to get back in." I stare at Daya. Tabia sobs. Then without warning, she lashes out and slaps Daya's cheek. I grab her around the waist and drag her backwards along the branch. She's fighting me and I'm struggling to keep my balance.

"Tabia! This isn't helping," I yell, still holding her tightly. "Stop. Please." My eyes are fixed on Daya, trying to understand. Her hand is pressed to her cheek and she's holding back tears. The sudden attack shocked her. "Why didn't you tell us sooner?"

I can hear the hurt in Sekani's voice as he demands a reason from me. The truth is, I don't have one. Not a good one anyway. I did come back yesterday as soon as I could get away from the camp, but there was nobody here again. And I came as soon as I could today. I just... I didn't know how to tell them. I didn't know what to say. I was afraid that they'd take it badly. And they have. Now I'm watching Tabia as her anger turns into grief and wondering how to make it better.

"Why didn't you tell us?" Sekani asks again. "Before it was too late."

"It's not too late," I say. Sekani looks at me and shakes his head. His empty laugh chills me. I've lost his trust.

"They're already marching, Daya. They'll be a long way round already and we don't even have a plan. It is too late."

Tears are still streaming down Tabia's ashen face and she starts to shake at Sekani's words. My lip begins to quiver too. They truly believe there's no hope and their sorrow is painful to watch.

"There's time. The men are going to march round the walls seven times today. They haven't even been round once yet." Two pairs of eyes are staring coldly at me. They show no sign of having heard what I said. I repeat my words. "There is still time."

It takes me a while to realise what Daya is saying. And even then, I don't fully understand. My mind is slow and heavy. Perhaps that's because I'm so upset already. "So what's the plan from here?" I'm giving Daya a chance. I feel angry. And hurt. And confused. *What are we going to do? What can we possibly do that we haven't tried already this week?* I think she wants to help. I just hope that she can, because I think Daya may now be our only hope of getting back home alive.

"I'm not sure what the longer march will do to their pace. And we need to know how people on the walls will react to the change. I hope they'll follow quickly when the procession moves further round the walls. But they may panic when Israel go around again."

"So what's the plan?"

"Did you two arrange for the rope to be dropped?"

"No! I told you. The king had his men out every time the Israelites left. We couldn't get close!"

"So what were you doing for the past couple of days? Where were you when I came yesterday?"

"Two days ago I was totally fed up. We'd run out of options and nothing was working. We stayed here. We spent the morning arguing with one another about what to do and whether you were coming back or not. We spent the afternoon sulking and ignoring one another. It was miserable."

"If you'd listened..."

"You didn't say anything useful."

"I might have..."

"You just kept putting my ideas down."

"I just wanted to point out—"

"All right. You both had a bad day," says Daya, putting an end to the conversation before things get worse. "I'm really sorry I couldn't get here earlier."

"Yes. It was a total waste of time. If I'd known then that today was going to be our last chance, I'd have tried much harder."

"And yesterday?" she asks carefully. She seems unsure whether her question was wise and braces herself for more bickering.

"We still couldn't agree," says Tabia. "I needed some space, so I went for a walk. I ended up back near your camp, watching. I told myself that if you weren't coming, I'd find the spies and get some answers. But—"

"When it came to it she wasn't brave enough to go in. And anyway, those men were probably part of the march, like I said in the first place. After she'd gone, I went back to the city again. I knew it'd be the same, but I hoped I'd see something, anything I hadn't noticed before that might help. Or overhear something."

"And did you?"

"No, I stayed well back in the field because the soldiers were out again - and on the walls too. I threw some stones at the window. I thought if I could get one through, someone in the house would at least know we'd been there. Most didn't even get close though. It's higher than I remembered. And one soldier was getting suspicious so I had to stop. I actually thought about letting them see me. They'd have taken me inside the walls before I knew it and I could have tried to escape from them there. I could have gone home and let the rope down and... I couldn't actually risk getting caught though - Tabia would have been totally alone if they'd got me."

"You didn't tell me..."

"It wasn't important."

"But it could have solved—"

"And it might have been a disaster. I stopped throwing stones, even though I was getting pretty close by then, because I didn't want to risk it, which was really annoying because someone came to the window just as I was leaving and I had no way to get their attention without the soldiers—"

"Someone was at the window?" Daya sounds surprised.

"Yes! I don't know who it was. I was too far away."

"At the window you left from? The one with the rope? And the red cord?"

"Yes, but I couldn't get very close. They didn't see us. Now we have no way—"

"Sekani, this is fantastic news!" My eyebrows rise with a question and I'm stunned.

What does she mean? How can this possibly be good? Sekani couldn't get their attention. No one is expecting us. No one is there to help us back in! After a long wait, Daya speaks again. "It means someone is looking for you," she explains. Clearly she thinks this is obvious, though I don't quite see how. "If they were just watching Israel or the soldiers, they'd have been on the walls with the others. They were at the window with the cord. Someone wants you back..." Well, maybe, but... "And if that's true, I'm certain they'll be there again today!"

Before I can wonder how she's so sure of all this, or ask how it's even helpful when we've still got to get to them, agree a plan and carry it out, we're interrupted by Sekani.

"Shh," he insists. "Listen!"

At first I don't hear anything, so I open my mouth to start arguing with Daya again. But the look of concern in Sekani's eyes makes me stop and glance towards the city. I concentrate hard on the sounds coming from that direction. I have to work hard to block out the dull roar of the Jordan and the rustling of leaves around me, but eventually I manage it and realise what my brother is saying. The sound of rams' horns and many feet stepping in time on the ground, which had faded away to nothing as Daya joined us and Israel marched onwards, is faintly audible again now. Have we been talking that long? It seems much too soon for a complete circuit of the city, but the crowds on the wall, who had left the northern section a while ago are quickly spreading back there again. The rhythmic thud, thud, thud of feet falling together is growing louder. Israel have really increased their pace today and judging by all the pointing and frantic conversation on the walls, the citizens of Jericho have noticed this too. It won't be long before Israel begin their second circuit!

"Daya, they're coming back! What are we—?"

"Let's go! We can't waste any more time sitting here, talking. We need to get closer – quickly!"

"She's right," I agree. "They're not going to wait for us."

"But we don't know what we're going to—" Tabia protests.

"We'll improvise," I insist. "By the time we have a perfect plan, it'll all be over."

"But..." she begins again. She seems very unsure about leaving the safety of the tree.

"Tabia, there's no time!"

"Come on," says Daya gently, seeing Tabia fight back tears. She's shaking a little too. We both want to be at home again, to see our family. And Tabia seems scared it won't happen, ever again. Daya squeezes her hand and looks straight into her eyes. "It's going to be all right, Tabia. We're taking you home now." I smile at Daya. In spite of everything, I'm glad she's here.

Together, we guide Tabia through the field. I'm not entirely sure how we got her down from the tree. It seemed to take forever. She wants to go home, but she's afraid of the journey. All I can think about is getting her safely back to our family. Her fear is making everything harder. Much harder. And slower. We're supposed to have more time, and a plan - that'd be a million times better - but we'll just have to get on with it now. We're stalking through the middle of a barley field towards the northern section of the wall and my brain is working harder and faster than ever before.

Those footsteps are resounding inside my head and body like a drum. *They're too close; much too close; too loud. Thud, thud, thump, thud, thump.* I tried to warn the others that they're coming, but Sekani says we've got plenty of time. *He doesn't know. He can't hear them. Thud, thud, thump, thud, thump. We're not safe. The rams' horns are sounding a warning. Long and loud. Taraaaaa, taraaaaa.* I clamp my hands over my ears to block the sound. We're not safe here in the field. *We have to stop. Why won't they stop? Why can't Sekani hear those footsteps? They're so loud.* And then I see it: the face at the window. And all I can do is stare back. The others are still pushing me onwards. My legs barely respond. They lock up and I lean back hard against the pressure Sekani's putting on my back. I want to stop and look. *We have to stop. Has she seen us? I'm not sure she has. I can see her, but I mustn't get any closer yet. The army are too close. Thud, thud, thump, thud, thump They're coming. Taraaaaa, taraaaaa.* I feel my body getting suddenly hot and heavy and darkness smothers me. The blood pulsing through my body is so loud it drowns out everything else. Louder and louder, closer and closer. *I run to the wall. The army are approaching fast. I'll be trampled! The face at the window disappears from view. It's too late. I'm too late!*

"Tabia!" I lean over as she slowly opens her eyes. She squints in the light. Tall stems of wheat are all glistening around us and it's strangely quiet. Tabia is lying on the ground; sweating and shaking and there are tears on her cheeks. "Tabia, are you…?"

"What happened?" She pulls herself up to a sitting position and casts around, still adjusting to the bright sunlight. "Where's Sekani? Are we too late?"

"I'm here." Sekani says, throwing himself down onto his knees beside his sister. "Are you all right? You fainted. I think you may have been hallucinating." He turns to me and adds

"I don't think she saw me. I did my best, but the army are passing now. I can't get close because of the dust. I couldn't just sit there. I had to come back and check on Tabia."

"Who? What's going on?" Tabia is trying to sit up, but she's too weak and I catch her as she trembles and collapses backwards again.

"Rest," whispers Sekani. Tabia tries to argue but isn't strong enough. She closes her eyes. I pull Sekani aside and hope that Tabia can't hear what I'm saying.

"Go back. You have to try again. I'll look after Tabia. Go to the very edge of the field. Wait until the army have passed and try again. You have to be seen. The first circuit's completed already. We'll come as soon as we can – when Tabia's strong enough. But you need to be absolutely certain she knows. You need to be sure the rope is ready to be let down. Talk to her if it's safe." Sekani nods his understanding but doesn't move. He's still looking anxiously at Tabia. "Go on, Sekani. You don't have long."

25

"... around the city..."

By the time I'm strong enough to get up again, I've lost track of time. I feel bleary-eyed. Have I been asleep? I'm not sure. I have no idea how long we have left. Daya offers me a pomegranate. I don't feel like eating and we don't have time to waste. I try to push up, but my head starts to spin again and I feel weak. My body won't cooperate. Daya holds out the pomegranate again as I give up and flop back to the ground. I sigh, but I take it from her outstretched hand and bite into the flesh. I immediately feel the juice cooling and calming me and have to admit she was probably right. I hurriedly chew through a few more mouthfuls until my body feels cool and my head stops pounding.

"Thanks." I smile at Daya.

"Do you feel better?" I nod and smile again. I do feel better. "Good. Sleep usually helps."

"Did I sleep? How long has it been? Daya! How could you let me sleep?"

"You needed to..."

"I can't believe—" I leap to my feet. We've got to—"

"Slow down. You still need to take it calmly." I shake my head in disbelief.

Then, still lost for words and without wanting to waste any more time, I set off towards the wall. I remember hearing Daya telling Sekani to go there. How can I be calm when we've wasted precious time? I turn to see Daya following. She still looks concerned about me, but I ignore it. I need to get to Sekani. I need to help him. The short trek seems to be taking forever. I pick up my pace.

I'm squatting near the edge of the field, peering out from between long, thin stalks. I smile as Daya and Tabia join me, but I don't say a word. I mustn't. I'm thankful that Tabia seems to have recovered. She sits down, being careful not to make a sound as she lowers herself to the ground. She slowly pushes away a few stems with the back of her hand to see out.

"Careful," I mouth. I gesture upwards. Tabia follows my gaze to the top of the stalks, where the crop has grown too big and bent over with the weight. This crop would normally have been harvested before now; it's past its best. But that's not what I want her to see. Even the tiniest movement of Tabia's hand against the stem is magnified, making the tops swing around freely in big sweeping waves. The movement could easily be seen from Jericho, or by passing Israelites. Tabia understands and immediately pulls her hand away. She sits as still as a carved sphinx guarding a temple. I want to laugh at her serious expression, but daren't.

"I don't know where she is," I whisper. "She was definitely here before. When I got back, the army were still passing and she'd disappeared from the window. She hasn't come back. All I can do is hide here and wait. I haven't moved. I haven't looked away. But she hasn't come back. I don't know what's going on." I hope I'm speaking calmly - I don't want to worry Tabia - but I'm beginning to panic inside. My eyes are fixed firmly on the empty window. There's nothing else we can do, except wait.

We wait. And wait. It's agonising. Nothing happens for what feels like an eternity. My legs are numbing and my neck is growing stiff from craning up towards the window. But I can't move. The walls are lined with people, watching and waiting for Israel's next appearance and the slightest movement now would reveal our position and get us in a lot of trouble. Just when my vision is beginning to blur and I think my legs have actually gone to sleep for good, it happens. My whole body, which has been tense and stiff, relaxes at once and I grin with relief. Beside the tiny fleck of red at the window, a face has appeared again. At last! We're saved. It's going to be all right. We're going to make it! The head is moving from side to side, slowly scanning the edge of the field. I scramble to get up and wave back, but Sekani throws out a hand to stop me.

"The walls!" he hisses. He's right. They're packed again now. People are jostling for space and the best views. How can we get ourselves seen by one person, without being seen by everybody else up there? I can't think of a way. I bite my bottom lip and stare up at the walls hoping that I'll think of something soon. But I'm distracted. The onlookers on the wall begin shifting their focus to the distance and pointing. Some are shouting; others are pushing for front positions; one or two are even beginning to fight among themselves. It's total chaos up there. But they've clearly seen something in the distance, which can only mean that Israel is on the way back for a third circuit of the city. How far away are they? How long do we have before they get here? How long before the face at the window disappears again? I look from Sekani to Daya. Both of them look blank. Neither of them seem to have any more idea than I do.

"We have to do something soon, before she disappears again," I whisper frantically. "She has to know we're here or we don't stand a chance."

"We can't do anything with all those people watching," insists Sekani. "It's too dangerous. We don't know for certain that she'll leave the window again."

"We can't take that risk. If she goes now..." I shudder.

"... she may not come back." Daya finishes my sentence for me. She leans forward. "I agree with Tabia," she says to

Sekani. "You have to take the opportunity while you have it. There may not be another chance and without the rope—"

"I know! I know! But..." It's an impossible decision and the pain of making it is written on my brother's face. His forehead is wrinkled in thought, his eyes are hard and his lips are tight. He looks at me in desperation. I shrug my shoulders hopelessly. I want to help, but what can I say? If we don't do something now, and she goes, then we have no rope and this task is over. If we do, and we're seen, it's all over too. We sit, unmoving, each lost in our own thoughts. The tension is unbearable.

The army are getting closer. I can't hear the marching this time, but that may be because the noise from the crowds has grown to such an unbelievable volume. I can hear the call of the rams' horns over the din of the crowds. I stare into the distance, straining to see how near Israel is. I'm trying with all my concentration to focus beyond the stalks, which are obscuring my view, so I squint. Suddenly my attention is diverted and I gasp. Sekani is taking an enormous risk. He's on his feet, waving his arms and jumping up and down. I grab his arm and try to pull him back down to the cover of the crops. The face is still at the window, but not looking this way. She's watching the army approach. Sekani shakes me off. He's determined to get his message across. He continues to wave his arms. I hold my breath. I want to look away, but I can't. The armed men are in sight now. The crowds on the wall are out of control with confusion and panic. Sekani is still standing, clearly visible to all. A reflex makes me clutch

Daya's arm and cling to it. My pulse is pounding through my temples. Then the face turns. She looks for a moment straight at Sekani, and then disappears. Sekani drops like a stone into water and the army are marching so close to where we sit that the dust they are kicking up gets into my eyes and my throat, making tears run down my face as I hold back from choking.

We sit for ages in the dust. It's in my eyes, making me blink and sending tears streaming down my grimy face. I rub them with my fingertips, but this just smears the dirt around and makes my eyes sting even more. I have one hand over my nose and mouth, trying to prevent the thick dust from getting in as I breathe. I consider backing away, further into the field, away from the churning cloud of tiny bits of earth and grain. I can't though. We're so close that the men would spot the movement straight away. *How long will we have to sit like this?* Tabia is giving little controlled coughs and clearing her throat a lot. The rough sounds are hidden by the noise of the marching, but she's clearly struggling to keep still and quiet. Sekani sits with his eyes and lips tightly closed, waiting patiently. I try to think of other things. I wonder where Gurion is – probably not too far away from us – which just ends up making me think again about the men passing and the dust they're kicking up. This is so horrible. I don't know how much longer I can bear it.

And then they're gone. The dust is settling and the crowds are dispersing and as I watch Tabia dab her wet eyes with the heels of her hands, I notice Sekani looking up to the window. I shuffle to get comfortable and gently rub Tabia's back. She's still coughing to clear the dust from her tickly throat.

"Is she there?" I ask Sekani.

"Not yet. And there are a few people still hanging around on the wall too. We'll have to wait a bit longer." And we do. We sit together and watch the walls, willing the last stragglers to move on so that we have a clear opportunity to cross the open ground. None of us move. None of us speak. The quiet is only broken by the occasional cough from Tabia. There's nothing for anyone to say until the time comes. We'll know when it is.

Something at the window catches my eye. Movement. I turn my head and see what I can only imagine is the coiled rope being waved around. She's trying to attract our attention. I inhale loudly. The outer wall is not totally clear. Although most people have left, following the parade or simply deciding that there's nothing left to see, a stubborn few are still standing there. Among them is one that looks like he may be a guardsman on patrol, keeping the crowds under control. I'm still holding my breath as Tabia grabs hold of my arm, eyes wide and lets out a little squeak.

Before I realise what's happening, Sekani's on his feet again. He's repeating his earlier performance: waving his arms and shaking his head and pointing urgently towards the top of the wall. I can't believe he's taking such a huge risk a second time. Before I even have chance to react, he's sitting beside me again, hidden from view. I sit, heart pounding, waiting to see if he was noticed. The guard turns his head briefly in our direction as though he'd noticed the movement, but soon looks away again. He must think he imagined it. That was close though.

Finally, the wall clears of people and the guard leaves his post. I wait a few more minutes, just to be certain the way is clear. Then I give the signal for the rope. I watch it bounce and jolt its way down, unwinding as it goes, with a strange mixture of relief and nerves. The opportunity we so desperately need has finally arrived, and yet I know we're not safe until we're actually through that window.

The rope stops a little way above the ground. I'd forgotten that I'd had to drop down. As the end swings back and forth, slowing to its final position, I try to work out how high it is. I turn to the girls.

"I can reach it. I'm sure I can."

"I don't know, Sekani." It's Tabia. She's nervous.

"I only need to grab the end with one hand and then I can scramble up. One good jump should be enough."

"But—"

"It's all right."

"Sekani, I—"

"I'm not going to leave you. You can grab hold of my ankles and I'll do the work until you can reach the rope. It'll be all right. Trust me." She sighs, but doesn't argue any more. I wait. I don't know what else I can suggest. We have to make it work. Eventually Tabia nods her agreement. I turn to Daya.

"Daya. Thank you." She shrugs. "Thanks for coming back."

"Yes," says Tabia. "I'm sorry I was angry this morning." She shuffles her feet. "We wouldn't have got here without your help."

"We wouldn't have even known until it was too late."

"It's—"

"Thank Gurion for us too. When you see him."

"I will." Tabia and Daya hug. I pat her arm and smile.

"You should go. We need to get up there before the army get back and there's nothing else you can do here now. Get back to the camp."

"Yes. I will. Bye Sekani." She takes Tabia's hand. "Tabia, you can do this." Tabia smiles. They hug again.

"Go carefully," I say and then turn back to the wall. I'm getting anxious now. We don't have time to waste. I hate just standing around when the soldiers are getting closer with every second. I need to climb this rope.

I watch Daya walk away from us, deeper into the barley field. When the disturbed stalks return to their position, I take a deep breath and turn back to face my challenge. Sekani has already gone! He's sprinting across the gap between field and wall and I suddenly feel very alone.

"Sekani!" I shout out. I can't believe he's gone! I break into a run and without stopping to check it's safe, I burst out of the field. I pump my legs as fast as they'll go and focus on Sekani. The short distance between us seems huge. I'm moving quickly but I'm much more alert than usual. I take in every detail: the solid grey stone of the wall ahead of us; the brilliant white of the slope around it; the burning heat of the sun out in the open; the crunching of the rough, dirty ground under my feet. I also notice the sour taste of sweat running from my face over my lips and the sound of my shallow breaths as I work hard to catch up. I am catching up. Sekani is on the slope that leads to the base of the wall now, and he's slowing. I'm getting closer. As I do, he begins to struggle more. *What's wrong?* It's not that steep and Sekani is the most agile person I know. He's halfway up the slope now, but has really slowed down. He's leaning forward from his waist, trying to keep the momentum and stretching his hands out in front for extra support if he needs it. I reach the base of the slope just as one foot slides out behind him and his body hits the ground hard. He claws at the ground with his hands, but can't find a grip and rolls back towards me. I try to stop in time. I turn to one side to try to avoid him, but it all happens too quickly and I trip over his leg and stumble.

"Ouch. What happened, Sekani?" He's sitting up, brushing white powder from his legs.

"This happened," he says and holds out a hand covered in more of the white powder. "The whole slope is covered in it. It must be a sort of defence." My eyes widen as a thought hits me.

"Sekani! I should have known about this. I think I slipped on it on our way out."

"Yes. Me too. I'd forgotten."

"I thought I'd landed on some loose stones or soil. I didn't think any more about it."

"I should have checked. It's quite clever actually," he says, examining the ground.

"So…" I almost don't want to ask the question. "What are we going to do?" He looks up.

"Keep trying!"

I sit at the base of the slope and watch as Sekani tries again and again to reach the top of the slope. He runs, he crawls, he takes sideways steps, he even sits down with his back to the wall and uses his hands and feet to help him shuffle up. Nothing works. Sometimes he hardly gets anywhere, sometimes quite close, but he doesn't make it to the wall. And even if he did, he's still got to jump for the rope. But Sekani's stubborn and he's not giving up. My heart sinks. I don't think he'll make it. I know even if he does, I won't. I rub away at the white powdery material, wondering whether it's possible to clear a narrow pathway. It's not. Although the surface is dusty, the white substance is solid underneath. *Plaster?* I hide my face in my hands and drop my head onto my knees. This was our chance. I feel – again – that our hope is gone. As Sekani walks past me to give himself a long run up, I admire him for attacking this problem for such a long time. Then a sudden thought kicks me into action. *How long is a long time? And when did we last see Israel?* I leap up and run straight into my brother. He's taken aback. He'd been totally focused on his target when my shoulder knocked into his side. I grab his arms and speak in a panic.

"Get her to haul that rope back up. Fast! And then hide. The army will be here soon." I'm already running towards the fields, leaving Sekani to wonder what just happened to him. "I'll be as quick as I can. Don't go anywhere," I call back over my shoulder and hope he understood everything I said.

I'm in no hurry to get back to the camp, so I'm ambling slowly along the path between the fields. There's nothing else for me to do there until the men get back. I'd rather be walking than sitting by the tent, waiting for news. There's no point hiding among the crops this time. The Israelite men are still marching, and the soldiers from Jericho are inside the city. I'm the only one here. Nobody's going to see me. The plains are all mine. It's a strange feeling actually, being in between. I don't like it very much. I was so involved, so much a part of the action. I felt the pressure and the excitement. I worried, planned and hoped too. But I can't be there to the end. My role is over. It's not that I want to be facing that climb. I don't. But… maybe I just wanted to see it; to know that my friends are safe. They'll be home by now, where they belong. It's not long since I left them, but I miss Tabia and Sekani already. I wonder if Gurion felt the emptiness too, when he was alone in his tent last week. Maybe. But he had today to look forward to. His moment. He's part of the action again now. In the very centre of it. Where's my place? I sigh. I don't want to feel sorry for myself, I just don't want to go home yet either.

A sudden swish of movement and the rush of swift footsteps in the barley field startles me. I freeze, not certain whether to run or hide. *Who is it? A soldier? From Jericho or Israel? And have they seen me?* I begin to back slowly away down the path, keeping my senses alert. The sound has stopped. Everything is quiet again. I pause too, listening hard. *Where are they? What are they doing?* I'm about to turn and run when a figure bursts out of the field. I scream. The blur of movement flings its arms around me. My arms are pinned to my sides and I can't move.

"Daya!"

"Tabia! What are you doing? Where's Sekani? I thought—"

"I'm so glad I found you. Come on."

"What's—?"

"Come on!" She's on the move again, dragging me by the wrist. "We need your help!"

Come on. Hurry up. I'm crouching at the edge of the field. The Israelite army are in sight again and the rope is still dangling out of the window. Slowly, slowly it's getting shorter as it's hauled back into the dark little room at the top of Rahab's house. The twisted cord moves upwards in short, jerky movements. It bounces and jolts all over the place as it goes. The army are approaching fast. They're eating up the ground ahead of them. Perhaps it's because I'm under pressure but they seem to be marching faster than before. They'll be here very soon. The rope is barely above head height now, and still in the line of vision. *Come on!* Once again, the whole situation is out of my control. There's nothing I can do except wait and pray that we won't be caught. I don't even know where my sister is. She said she'd be back. *Is it high enough now?* It's hard to tell. My knee is jiggling and it's making it hard to focus. I try to steady my leg, but it's hopeless. I need to do something. I can't bear sitting here, watching. I can see the feet of the first row of soldiers now, marching in step, dusty, dirty, scratched and sore. Not wanting to be choked in their dust a second time, I crawl backwards deep into the field with only one last glance up at the dangerously dangling rope.

26

"... seven times."

I'm thirsty. No, I'm gasping. We're just beginning our fourth circuit of these walls and the pace has been harsh. I thought I was quite fit, but I'm tired and I'm sweating and my breathing is annoyingly fast. I can't even hide it because we're marching in silence – total silence! Nobody has said a single word. We're not allowed to. So the other men around me can hear exactly how out of breath I am. It's embarrassing. I've tried to distract myself from the effort by counting, humming in my head and even day-dreaming about tonight's meal, but most of the time I've been wondering how Daya and the others are getting on. I'm trying not to worry. There's nothing I can do to help them now, but I'd love to know whether they've made it back inside the walls yet.

I'm dropping behind again. *Step, two, step, four, step, six, step, eight, step...* I must keep pace with the other men. *Only four more times round. You can do this, Gu. ... step, 20, step, two, step, four...* As we head northwards again, I scour the fields near the marked window for signs of the others. Nothing. I don't know whether to be pleased – *they're being careful to stay hidden* – or worried – *what if they haven't arrived yet? ... step, eight, step, 40, step two...*

We're nearly at Sekani and Tabia's house again now. A few more steps and... *What? No!* I stare at the wall. My feet stop moving. Two or three soldiers bump into me from behind and others veer round the chaos, scowling fiercely at me. I hurriedly scramble back to my place and mouth "Sorry". As soon as I've picked up the rhythm of the march again, I look back over my shoulder to the window. And there it is – the rope! It shouldn't be hanging there like that now. It's going to be seen! I begin to panic, not knowing what to think. *What does this mean? What's happening?* I force myself to keep moving forward, away from the window and the rope, away from the answers to my questions. I can't risk drawing more attention to it. They may already be in trouble and I don't want to make it any worse.

I start to kick hard at the ground with every step I take. I'm taking out my frustration as I stride onwards. Eventually, after covering a lot of ground, I calm down and realise that it's a good sign: they probably just ran out of time to haul the rope in completely behind them, but that means they're actually inside the house. Excellent! If it's gone next time around, I'll know I was right. And that gives Daya plenty of time to get safely back to the camp too. This thought seems to re-energise me and I feel suddenly less tired. I start to look forward to the climax of all this marching and smile at the thought that I'm here: a part of this great story!

Over, under, over, round and back… I look up briefly as Tabia dumps another handful of barley stems onto the pile beside me. I nod, but don't speak. I need to concentrate. *Under, over, under…* I'm in a good rhythm now but it's going too slowly. Every time I try to speed up, I get in a muddle and that's even worse. It's better to work steadily. We've made a really good start, but this could take a while and time is running out. Every time something like this happens, it seems less and less likely that Tabia and Sekani will get home. But they're determined, and I won't give up either. We've got this far. So, I'm sitting cross-legged in the field, weaving stalks of barley to make a sort of mat. There's no grip on the slope, so we're going to provide some. It's a bizarre idea, I know, but it's the best one we have at the moment and doing something keeps the sense of panic away. Sekani is standing at the base of the slope, thinking. He's determined to beat it. He looks up. Instinctively, I do too. The guard is back on the wall above the window. Sekani won't be able to see him, but I can quite clearly. It's odd; the army passed a while ago – but they won't be back yet – and there's nobody else up there for him to keep an eye on. Tabia sits down beside me, lays out a few strands in parallel lines and begins work on another section. Her face shows how hard she's concentrating to get this done quickly. I pick up the next stalk and overlap it with my previous one. Over, under, over, under…

Tabia is holding back tears. I'm not sure how much more disappointment she can take. She's doing everything she can to help us get to that window, and so am I, but as she watched all her effort go to waste, her bottom lip began to tremble. The girls' mat did provide some grip for my feet and might have been a very good solution - except that as we had no way of securing it to the slope, as soon as I stood on it, it slid straight out from underneath me making me fall flat on my face. My cheek still stings. But that doesn't matter. What's worse is seeing my sister work so long and hard on her plan only to watch it fail.

A sharp whistling sound grabs my attention moments before I see the rope sailing from the window in a wide arc. The coil unravels quickly and drops heavily back into place against the wall. I stare at it, not understanding - or believing - what I see. Before, the rope had ended a little way up the stony face of the revetment wall, beyond the peak of the plaster slope. Now, it extends to the ground. The ground at the base of the slope!

"Daya, look!" She casts around, not realising what I'm talking about. "Up there. They've found more rope! I can see the knot where they've joined the pieces together." I throw my arms wide and hug Daya. She grins.

"That's fantastic!" As the words leave her mouth though, I notice a major problem.

"Sekani, let go!" I yell. "Now!" He looks stunned. He's halfway up the slope, using the rope to haul himself up – and he hasn't let go. He's just staring at me in disbelief. "Let go!" I repeat. "Sekani! You have to…"

I watch in horror as he releases the rope and topples backwards. His shoulder hits the ground first and his legs carry on moving up and over his head. He tumbles backwards down the slope. His limbs bash again and again against the ground. He ends in a crumpled heap. I run towards him.

"Ouch!" he says as he sits up. "Tabia, what was that about? Look what you've done to me!" He's covered in dust and he's going to be bruised all over. I bite my lip before I realise that he's actually teasing me. He notices. Then he laughs. "I'm fine. It wasn't that bad. Now what—"

"The rope. The knot. It…" I struggle to explain. Sekani looks up and knows straight away from the mass of frayed and broken strands that form the join that it wouldn't have taken his weight much longer. I can tell from the stunned sorrow in his eyes that he also understands if he'd been further up when it gave way, the fall could have been much, much worse.

"Thank you, Tabia," is all he manages to say before he squeezes my shoulder and walks away to have some time to himself. It's unlike Sekani, but I think this shock really upset him.

I let him go. He'll be fine – and he'll be back. And I have something I need to do before then.

Sekani grabs the rope firmly with both hands and begins to scale the wall. He scuttles like a scarab beetle, using all four limbs to propel himself. The face in the window is willing him on. I stand rooted to the spot at the edge of the field, watching his progress, not daring to move or breathe.

Thanks to Tabia's quick thinking, they have another opportunity now. I'd been ready to give up the quest and take them both back to Gilgal. I know how foolish that would have been. They wouldn't exactly have been made welcome, but the situation here was impossible. At least, I thought so. I couldn't see any other way. But in spite of everything she's been through today, Tabia was clear-headed enough to spot a small detail that turned everything around. She explained to me that with the shorter section of rope attached to the window at the top, the knot would have to hold their weight until they'd scaled most of the way up the mud-brick surface. The risk was much too big, as Sekani had just proved. "But, If the shorter section is at the bottom…" she said, beaming with excitement at her own suggestion.

"… It only has to hold you until you're just beyond the slope. And if you fell from there…"

"We'd survive," she finishes with a satisfied nod.

Communicating the plan from our position on the ground was challenging to say the least. The distance is too great to speak and be heard, and shouting is not a safe option. We had to rely on gestures and mime. And, in the middle of all that, we had to scramble back into the field and let the whole of Israel's procession march past us once again. They're on lap five now. It seems like only minutes ago I was scrambling up the trunk of the fig tree. And at the same time, so much has happened, this morning seems like a distant memory. Time is doing very odd things today.

As Sekani reaches the top of the stone retaining wall, I reflect on the great distance between him and the ground. He's a long way up and seems unaware of the danger. But if he fell… Tabia is clutching my arm. She is swaying a little and I wonder if she's going to faint again. What is she thinking now this whole adventure is nearly over? Relief? Tiredness? Fear? She seems terrified watching Sekani dangling so casually from the rope, but to get home she's going to have to climb it as well.

Sekani has paused to look back and check what's going on and I realise that Tabia is not going to go. She's still clinging to me. I shove her hard in the back, propelling her towards the wall and the end of the rope. She's shaking a little as she takes hold of it. I take a deep breath. Tabia doesn't move. *Come on, Tabia. You can do this.* She finally places a foot on the slope and pulls hard against the rope but as she steps forward with her other foot, the first slips back down behind her. Her knees land heavily on the ground and she loses her balance. I close my eyes and take a deep breath in. *Try again, Tabia. Don't panic. Take it slowly.* She quickly scrambles to get up and looks back over her shoulder to where I'm watching from the field. I nod, and signal for her to try again. She takes hold of the rope in both hands, places one foot on the slope once more and takes a deep breath. But her confidence is shaken and it takes Tabia another few minutes to progress any further. She simply stares up at the wall, looking up its face to the distant fleck of red, awestruck by the task. And Sekani is waiting. He's willing her on and I know if it wouldn't get them caught, he'd be shouting encouragement. Cautiously, Tabia heaves herself back onto the rope and begins to climb. Every nervous step is testing her courage. It looks as though each movement is a huge effort for her.

After a very short time climbing, my arms feel too weak to support my body any more. My legs are shaking. My mind is swirling. I look up to Sekani, who's waiting for me halfway up the rope. He's still much too far away. I look down to see how far I've come. It's further than I thought – I'm doing better than I realised – but this doesn't motivate me. Looking down was a mistake. A big mistake. My stomach lurches violently and churns like the Jordan in flood and my foot slips suddenly off the wall. I tighten my grip on the rope, but my strength fails me and I slide down a short distance, stinging my hands and scraping layers of skin off my knee. My heart pounds against my chest and I look to Sekani. His face reflects my fear and suddenly it's all too much. I don't think I can do this. I can't go any further. Despite my shaky position, I begin to cry.

Tabia's tears haven't stopped since she lost her footing and now she's shaking uncontrollably on Daya's shoulder. I made my way back down the rope to Tabia as quickly as I could, but I couldn't really help much from above; I didn't want to risk another accident. Thankfully, Daya scrambled up to help Tabia down from the rope and led her back to the cover of the crops but now they're just standing there, not saying a word. I should've known she'd find this hard. I didn't think. I could have helped her. I need to talk to my sister; to reassure her; to apologise. I should have helped more. I look at Tabia. Poor girl. She probably thinks it's her fault. I shouldn't have pushed her so hard. I shouldn't have rushed her. She must be feeling terrible now. I don't speak, but sweep Tabia's hair away from her wet face. As I'm hopelessly wondering what I'm going to do next, Daya suddenly pulls away from Tabia and tenses up.

"Daya? What's wrong?"

"What? No, it's nothing." She doesn't look at me while she's speaking. "Don't worry."

"Daya, is something wrong? What's happening?" She shakes her head, but still doesn't look me in the eye.

"Stay with Tabia. And sit down. You... you both need a rest. I'll be back." She walks away from us, staying in the field and moving parallel to the city walls. *What's going on? Is the stress too much for Daya now too?* I don't think I can cope with two weeping girls.

I sit down on the ground and sigh heavily. We were so close. This couldn't have gone more badly wrong - and it's all my fault.

That was much too close. As I stood comforting Tabia, something caught my eye. Something on the wall. The guard was talking to another man, probably another guard, who looked as though he'd just arrived in a hurry. I left so I could keep an eye on them without worrying Sekani or Tabia any more. Not much happened. They talked for a while. I'm sure the first pointed in our direction, but the other seemed to laugh and shook his head. We seem to be safe for now, but they're both standing guard and at least one of them may suspect something. We have to be careful. I ease my way back through the barley, disturbing the stalks as little as I can.

Sekani is holding his head in his hands and Tabia is whimpering feebly beside him. I hesitate, not sure what to say. If they go soon, they'll still have time to attempt the climb again. But I don't think they will. In front of me sit two people who've already decided that they've failed. They don't see that there's still an opportunity to succeed. They don't realise that there's still time; they have another chance. They'll have to go soon, and they'll have to move when the guards are distracted. I open my mouth to speak, but hesitate again. I need to be careful what I say next. If I get it wrong… No, that's a bad way to look at it. If I get this right, Tabia and Sekani still stand a chance of surviving the day. I mutter a quick prayer under my breath and hope for the best. I can't waste any more time waiting and wondering.

Daya is ready to go back to the camp. We're watching Israel approach – this is the last but one circuit. There's not much time left and the real action of the day will begin; whatever that might be. I don't know what to expect after the final circuit, but whatever happens, it's going to be significant. I'm quite excited now. Still nervous, particularly as there's still a lot for Sekani and me – especially me – to do, but as Daya rightly pointed out, "It's not over yet". I'm really glad she was there. I felt like a total failure and Sekani had given up hope too. If we'd been alone, the two of us would still be sitting here when… Well, when it happens. Now I realise how stupid that would be – to sit back and wait to die. Climbing that wall may be the most difficult challenge we've faced since leaving Jericho, but it's not impossible. There's still a chance we can get there. I have to remember that. I have to believe it. I have to try. Before I can though, we've got to get Daya back to her rightful place. They're returning to begin the sixth circuit and we can't risk leaving it any later. Daya needs to be in Gilgal every bit as much as we need to be inside that wall. Her safety depends on it and after everything she's done, I owe her the opportunity to go. If I don't make it home in time, I'll know that she has. Gurion and Daya have become great friends and supported us this far, but the last obstacle is something Sekani and I have to face together. We got ourselves out, and we need to get ourselves back in. Together.

"Are you ready?" It's Sekani. Daya doesn't say much. She nods without even looking round. She's deep in thought. "Thank you," he says softly. This time she does look around, and smiles.

"Look after each other," she says. It's my turn to smile.

"Yes," I reply.

But Daya doesn't go. She stands beside us in silence watching the last of the army pass by. I take a deep breath. It's my turn next. My chance to get myself back where God wants me to be. Moments away. I'm scared. This is the last chance I'm gong to have. I hope I'm not too late to succeed.

"Let's go," whispers Sekani as the dust settles behind the last of Israel's people. "You go first. I'll be right behind you. Take your time and don't look down." I nod and look up at the window. "Tabia," he says. "Focus on the scarlet cord."

"No!" The yell takes me by surprise. I'd been so focused on what I needed to do, I'd forgotten Daya was still there. "Run!" Before I have time to think, Daya has grabbed my hand and yanked me round to face the other direction. I see fear in her eyes. *What...* She runs, and I have no choice but to follow. My body gets ahead of my feet and I nearly fall, but somehow I keep my balance, plunging on through the field. Tabia's just behind me, keeping up as well as she can. I can hear her footsteps and the swish of the barley stems, and I can almost smell her fear. I don't know what we're running from, but Daya doesn't slow down so neither do I.

"Daya..." I puff.

"Guards."

"But..."

"They saw us. They're coming. See that tree? Ahead of us, to your right?" I takes me a while to find the tree she means. We're still running hard so the view is jumping around behind a blur of golden shoots.

"Yes."

"Climb it. Wait until the danger has passed. Then go back and get yourselves in."

"What are you going...?" She stops running and looks at me.

"We lured them away before they spotted the rope, but they're not far behind. Go! I'm going to distract them. Keep them away as long as I can."

"Daya, you can't. They'll—"

"Go, or we'll all be caught!" This time it's Tabia who grabs my hand. As we run towards the tree, I hear Daya's voice again, singing. It's calm and sweet in the middle of all this stress and confusion. My heart almost breaks. She's doing this to save us. *Please don't find her. Let her be safe.*

27

"Shout, for the Lord has given you the city."

This time we're not taking any chances. Tabia is ahead of me so that I can talk her through every move she needs to make. She's not trying to do this on her own now. Even so, I'm impressed that she's calm as we approach the wall. Tabia hates climbing; we have an impossibly short time to scale the heights of the towering wall - the same wall that's defeated her once already today - and after this there are no more chances for us. Israel's soldiers finished their sixth lap while we were creeping back from our hiding place in the tree, terrified that the guards would appear from nowhere and seize us. So, this is it. We get to the window and we live. Or we don't and... and we... Considering all that, she's staying very relaxed. Or seems to be. I can't tell what's going on beneath the surface.

"Are you ready to go?" I ask, pushing thoughts of Daya's safety from my mind. There's nothing I can do about that now. I only pray she kept well hidden. We've paused at the top of the slope, looking up towards the window. It's so high, we're so close and there's so much wall in between that I can't actually see the window or even the red cord. There's no answer from Tabia. She's staring at the rope, lost in thought. I wait. I don't want to seem impatient, but I'm worried. We *need* to get started. And the more she stands here thinking, the more likely it is she'll start to panic again. "Tabia? Are you ready?" I take the rope in one hand and fidget with the end. *Come on. We've got this far. You can't stop now.* "Tabia!" I notice the impatience creeping into my voice and bite my tongue. I'm torn. My every instinct is to grab the rope - push my sister ahead of me and scream at her to climb - I can't bear standing here not doing anything when the army are getting closer every moment. But I know if I do, it'll make things worse. She's a thinker, a planner - but not a doer. Tabia needs reassurance, encouragement - I should say something that will convince her not to be scared. But I don't know what. I notice that I'm fiddling frantically with the rope, twisting and turning it in my palm. I wish Daya hadn't left. She'd know what to say. *Please, Tabia. We can't stay here. It's too dangerous.* I wonder how far the Israelites have gone and how long it will take me to move Tabia. Will there be enough time left? I know that I could do it quickly - and under pressure, but I'm not convinced that Tabia can. I put a hand on Tabia's back and speak as gently as I can. "Come on. Let's go."

"Yes. I'm ready now." Her voice is a whisper. It wavers a little, but she's being brave. I hand her the rope and watch as she carefully lifts her arms as high as she can and pulls her body upwards. Her feet scrabble around for a foothold on the wall.

"Try holding the rope between your feet instead." I suggest. "You might be able to grip it better." She tries and after one or two attempts manages to secure the rope.

"What now?"

"Move each hand in turn, then shuffle your feet up." Tabia manages to move her hands up the rope a little, crossing one over the other, but loses her grip on the rope as she follows with her feet.

"Sekani!" she yelps in panic.

"It's all right," I say, as calmly as I can. This could take much more time than we have. I steady the rope so that she can find it again. "Now try that again... good. But don't take your feet off the rope! Just loosen your grip enough to slide them up. Perfect." She managed that well and repeats the sequence, moving her hands first, one over the other, and then sliding her feet. It's working, but it's painfully slow and very erratic. "Tabia," I call up to her, "I'm going to start climbing now. You're going to feel the rope moving a bit - I'll keep it as steady as I can. Just keep going like you are - you're doing really well."

"I'm scared, Sekani. It's too far."

"You're doing a great job. You just need to find a rhythm and keep moving. Don't look down and don't stop." I launch myself onto the rope behind my sister and place my feet firmly against the wall. I lean back, supporting my entire weight with my hands, hoping this will create some tension in the rope and make it easier for Tabia to climb. I don't speak any more. I want her to concentrate on every movement. I stay close enough to reassure her. Not too close though. If she does slip again, I'll need time to react.

The stone wall feels solid against my feet and the rough rope fits snugly in the palms of my hands. The twisted cords are frayed and rough, but strong too. Going at Tabia's pace, I have plenty of time to examine it as I move it slowly through my hands. It's incredible that something so strong was made by combining small strands. A bit like us meeting Gurion and Daya, I realise. I know Daya has given Tabia the strength to climb again, and without Gurion we wouldn't have known Israel's plans for today. We've had much more success with their help than trying to save our entire family by ourselves. *Where are the guards? Is Daya still safe?*

I look up. We're about halfway up the retaining wall now. The one that holds back the hill that supports the whole city of Jericho. I can see where it stops and the mud-brick wall begins. But it's still quite far away, and although Tabia has found a sort of rhythm - she's chanting quietly to herself as she makes each move - it's still very slow. And I know that when we reach that point, we still have the outer wall of our house to climb. *Come on, Tabia. Hurry up. This isn't fast enough.*

"You're doing really well, Tabia. We're making good progress."

Where are Israel's soldiers? How long have we got? I strain my ears to listen, but the noise of the crowds on the wall drowns out everything else. The higher we climb, the louder they get. I'm not sure if that's because we're closer, or because Israel is. I wish I could see what the people on the wall can see. I wish I knew how much time is left.

"I'm proud of you. Just keep your rhythm going."

We've got a long way to go. We'll be too late! How can I get her to climb faster? I don't want to worry her - she's concentrating hard on climbing the rope - but I don't think we're going to be there in time. If I tell her that, she'll panic, and then it'll all be over. I listen hard again. There's nothing except Tabia's muttering and the heckling of the slum dwellers on their roofs. *If they were close, would I hear them? Or will they just arrive beneath us without warning.* I lean back as far as I dare, craning my neck to see into the distance. Tabia squeaks. I've frightened her. She's stopped climbing and is clinging for her life.

"Sorry." I can hear her breathing, shallow and fast. I carry on straining to see what's going on below us. "That was my fault. You're doing really well." She doesn't move. "Go on, Tabia. I'm here - just behind you." Still she clings to the rope, not daring to move. I've got to distract her - focus her on reaching the cord again. "Just start with one hand. Like before. Lift it over the other." She does. "And the other one. Good." *Wow. That was close. I thought it was all over.* "Now feet, hand, hand..." *Can I get her to speed up? I have to try.* "... hand, feet, hand, hand, feet, hand... Great, Tabia! Perfect!" We're moving again. We're on mud-brick now and making good progress. The window is in sight!

I have no concept of time any more. I know that it's running out with every step closer we get to the window. The faint sound of a ram's horn reaches my ears. It's a long time since the soldiers passed us for the final time. *How long has it taken us to get this far? Where are the soldiers?* We're so close, but Tabia is shaking now. She might even be crying. *How much time is left? Is it enough?*

My thoughts are interrupted abruptly by a din that makes the clamour of Jericho's citizens on the walls seem like a mere whisper. I startle and the rope jerks. Tabia gasps. Her legs flail. Shouting? It's shouting! Hundreds and hundreds of people are shouting together. It's a battle cry. An army ready to attack.

Israel!

28

"The wall fell down flat."

My body tenses with shock: my back straightens and my eyes pop open. The sheer force of the sound stuns me. I'm hiding out in a sycamore tree much further around the wall from where I left, waiting until it's safe to go home. After a morning of hearing only the dull thud of feet and the muted, breathy tones of the rams' horns from Israel, the sound of human voices shouting in unison comes as a total shock. I wasn't expecting such volume, such passion, such strength and depth and unity. It's as though the sound was created by some monstrous mythical creature, not many weak, inexperienced individuals.

The sound comes as a shock to the Canaanites too. Israel are standing close to the main gate to the great city of Jericho. The army has stopped marching and turned as one to face the walls. My position gives me a good vantage point of the army – and the citizens on the rooftops. The sudden change of behaviour has confused and scared them. The jostling and bickering has stopped. The gossiping and fighting has stopped. The people on the walls stand as still and silently as if they were statues. Many are open-mouthed. All are wide-eyed. The strange image fixes itself in my mind and I know I'll be able to remember it clearly for years to come. It vanishes before I know it though. It doesn't last more than a few seconds before everything is thrown into chaotic action once more. The shouting tails off; the echo from the wall dies away. There's a moment of terrifying silence as everyone wonders what's going to happen next. Everything after this seems to happen very slowly, but it's all over in a matter of moments.

The first thing I notice is the red bricks of the upper wall shifting slightly backwards and forwards. The movement is tiny at first and I'm sure I'm imagining it. I'm not. Soon the wavelike ripple is spreading along the wall, growing bigger and bigger as it travels. It reminds me of leaves in the breeze. But it doesn't stop there. There's an unsettling "crack" as a fracture appears in one of the bulges and quickly spreads, zigzagging its way up and down the wall. I watch wide-eyed as more cracks appear. Then, unexpectedly, I wobble violently. I flail my arms out, instinctively grabbing hold of a branch to steady myself. The ground is shaking with a low rumbling sound. The growl grows louder as the whole plain trembles. I watch as a red brick lands with a thump and shatters into several pieces at the foot of the plaster slope. The rumbling and cracking is joined by anxious shouts from the wall as people there cling to one another in fear, scrabbling to find a safe place to stand. I brace one foot against the trunk to steady myself and stand rooted, staring at the people on the walls. Their mouths are opened in screams but the sound doesn't reach my ears any more over the swelling sounds of destruction all around. It's the most disturbing thing I've ever seen. I think of Sekani and Tabia and their family and I feel sick. *Where are they?* If they're on the wall, they won't stand a chance now.

I blink. The screaming faces are fading into the distance. I strain my eyes to see; to work out what's happening. A haze of dust is rising from the ground. Each time a chunk of wall plummets to the ground it sends a large cloud into the air. And they're falling faster now. Bigger and bigger chunks of wall are breaking off. Whole segments are crashing down. My hand flies to my mouth. I gasp. Somebody is tumbling from the top of their roof. Their arms are outstretched as they fall, down and down... I cover my eyes. I can't watch. A scream rings out over the chaos and I squirm uncomfortably, unable to block out the image of what's happening. Then suddenly it stops. It's over. The person is dead. There's no doubt in my mind. No one could have survived that fall. The sick feeling in my stomach returns. I retch and bend my head low over a branch. I don't vomit. I wish I had. Then the queasy churning in my stomach might have stopped. The terrible sounds continue for what seems like forever, before they slowly, slowly fade; and then the silence afterwards seems so unnatural.

I take a few deep breaths and push myself up. I watch as the dust gradually settles and stand staring at the wreck. Jericho's redbrick wall lies in an untidy heap only metres in front of me. Unbelievably, the wall has collapsed outwards. Many of the citizens are already dead. Their corpses lie scattered among the bricks and boulders. They've fallen from the wall or been crushed in the chaos. My head is spinning and spiralling and only one thought remains.

Where are Tabia and Sekani?

29

"They took the city."

On the officers' command, we march. We march straight forward: towards what remains of the great city of Jericho. Directly ahead of me is a heap of broken redbrick and earth. Mingled into the mess are the shattered remains of people's homes. The houses that had been built against the outer wall have collapsed with it and their contents scattered in the devastation. Everything from bundles of barley to earthenware and furniture can be seen strewn among the debris, broken and battered, twisted and torn. It's the most mess and mayhem I've ever seen.

So much damage has been done and so much debris has fallen that the stone wall holding back the hill itself is no longer visible. The landslide of brick and mud from on top has spread out from the city boundary so that if forms a ramp all the way from street level down to the surrounding plains where I stood watching the nightmare happen. Now we're marching, we've quickly reached the edge and are picking our way over the loose debris at the foot of the mound; the bits that slid furthest and rolled longest. I soon pass through this, kicking things aside and crushing them underfoot, and step onto the newly created slope.

The slope itself is uneven and extremely dangerous. I slow down to pick my way over odd lumps and step over potholes. Once or twice, I stumble as I step on a brick or plank that works loose. Still I march onwards and upwards, straight ahead, shoulder to shoulder with the armed men. It's a great feeling, to be part of this team; part of this story. I did the right thing going back to Dad and I made the right decision. This feels right. It's where I belong.

Despite that, this is not the nicest experience of my life. On the street above me, people are running this way and that in total panic. Some are heading for the inner walls in search of safety. Others charge down the slope in the vain hope of dodging past our men and escaping into the fields. They don't succeed – they are killed with the sword and their lifeless bodies join the other casualties on the mound, sprawled out, trampled and abandoned. It's a horrible way to die. Those who chose to hide will be found too. No living thing, young or old, human or animal will survive the day. God has given Jericho to Israel.

I step cautiously over the twisted limbs of an earlier fatality and I'm suddenly overwhelmed with the desire to kick something. *Why? Why do they have to die like this? I'm angry. Is this what it means to be a man? To do these unthinkable things to others – others like Sekani and Tabia* – others like us. I feel like stopping here in protest; refusing to go on. But a dim memory stirs. *What did Dad say?* "Not because of our righteousness, but because of their wickedness." I don't fully understand what that means but I know this is the way God planned it. I'm one of his people now – marked out. I don't want to live by my own rules any more. I trust him to lead me well. I step over the corpse of a small child and look away, putting the image immediately out of my mind. I raise my sword and step onto the street that circles around the inner wall. I'm inside the city boundary: inside the walls.

30

"They burned the city with fire."

On the hill to the west of the River Jordan, a raging fire burned. The blaze consumed an area the size of a large city. Fierce tongues of flame danced and leapt high into the night air. The bright light flickered and flared and lit up the landscape for miles around. The crops in the fields wilted in the intense heat. Thick smoke filled the air, depositing layers of ash across the plains. The stench of burning flesh was repulsive. Abundant springs of cool, fresh water that had irrigated the crops and nourished a nation did not quench the flames. They could not. The inferno was too hot; too fierce; unstoppable.

Before setting light to the wreckage on the great heap of bricks that once stood tall and proud, the Israelites had removed most items of value. The mighty strength of Jericho had been overcome. Now its considerable wealth was being stripped away too. The gold and silver the Israelites found was gathered together in one place and added to the Lord's treasury. Any items made from iron and bronze were collected and put there too. Tools and utensils, ornaments and jewellery were all removed from the territory. Everything that had once made Jericho great was no more.

Now Jericho was on fire. The great walled city was being destroyed. The Israelites had slaughtered every living thing with their swords. Men and women, young and old, sheep, ox and ass had been killed. No living thing within the walls had been spared. The devastation was complete; total; absolute. Now everything that remained of the once great state of Jericho was being burned.

When the fire had finally burned itself out, the ash had settled and the smoke dispersed, Jericho was left in a state of carnage. Every room in every house was filled with fallen bricks. Walls were blackened, floors were scorched, possessions destroyed. Anything that remained intact had been buried in the rubble or coated in smouldering ash. Jars, full to the brim with grain gathered in to help Jericho survive the siege, had been toppled over, spilled or smashed. The land was unrecognisable. The city and everything in it did not exist any more.

With one exception: on the northern section of the outer wall, a small portion of mud-brick wall still stood, oblivious to the devastation around it. The house built against it had withstood both the tremors in the ground and the vibrations through the wall; it was undamaged by the earth and brick and household objects that had plummeted and smashed and pummelled the ground all around it; untouched by the armed men who stormed the city to destroy it. Now, it alone towered above the plains. A single surviving structure in a vast scene of ruin and wreckage. It was the only landmark for miles around, and in its window a tiny sliver of bright red was visible: a tribute to the faith and courage of those who had once lived there.

31

"As you have sworn."

We're sitting outside the camp-ground at Gilgal, listening to the rush of the River Jordan and surveying the scene that lies in the distance across the plains. I can't tear my eyes away from the sight of the house where I know the scarlet cord still hangs. It's no more than a minute fleck of colour but it stood out in the mass of greys and browns that surrounded it. Now, it could be the only colour that remains in what was once Jericho. The glimmering golden colour of the barley has been erased, smothered by the thick layer of ash that fell; the lush green of the palms and figs wiped out as the leaves wilted and shrivelled in the heat; the sparkling blue of the streams replaced with a dirty, muddy brown from the pollution. That little piece of cord could be the only hint of colour that has survived in the desolate landscape.

And we are the only people to have survived the attack. Tabia sits beside me a little way off from the rest of our family. They are grouped together, facing away from their old home, focusing instead on the refreshing water of the river and the homely campground of Israel at Gilgal. Soon, we will join them. But for now, I need to be here; to take in the scene; to look back and reflect on how close I came to being destroyed with the rest of the city. Tabia stares at the wreck too and I know her thoughts are similar to my own. We don't speak. There are no words to describe the feelings I have. I'm more than relieved, more than grateful, more than any words can describe. The sadness and regret is deeper than any I've experienced before, but so is the joy and excitement. I can't explain the way I'm feeling, I can't even make sense of it myself; but as I sit here, silently thanking the Lord of Israel for sparing my life, I feel a sense of peace in my heart more real than anything else I've ever felt. I know that everything is going to be fine now. I turn to my sister and smile. She returns the gesture. We're in the right place. I sense it and Tabia does too.

Before the shout of Israel's army had faded away, I had scrambled up the last short section of rope and shoved Tabia towards the window opening. Rahab and my mother were there to haul her in. They'd been waiting. I found out later that they'd been taking turns to stand at the window every day, checking for signs of us in the fields and plains, praying for our safety and that we would return. I clambered through behind her, abandoning the rope and falling onto the hard floor of the small upstairs room. For a long time, that's exactly where I stayed. The four of us sat holding each other. There were tears of relief and strong hugs expressing the love, apologies and forgiveness we were all too emotional to voice. Then for a long time we clung to one another in fear as the sounds from outside bombarded us. We didn't know what was happening. We didn't know what to expect. The rest of the family joined us and we waited. Waited for whatever was going to happen to us next. We listened as the wall collapsed and the people screamed and scrambled around in terror. We listened as the army approached. We listened to the sounds of the end of the world - or so it seemed.

Then, the spies burst through the door and pulled us to our feet. They led us out of the house and onto the street and down the mountain of rubble. Behind us, the rest of Israel's army marched on towards the city. I looked back over my shoulder and saw them advancing through the slums to the inner city, to the heart of Jericho. Their swords were raised. We continued as quickly as we dared, down through the rising dust to the plains. I couldn't process the sights that met my eyes; couldn't make sense of how something so strong had been so rapidly destroyed; couldn't believe that what I was seeing was real. We reached the bottom of the hill and walked on. We kept walking. Away from the carnage. Away from the city. Towards safety and security. And the unknown.

As we walked on, the air filled with thick black smoke and my nostrils were hit with the foul smell of burning. I looked back and saw the flames. The fire spread quickly and the blaze grew taller. I soon felt the heat on my back, and the spies walked faster. I was torn between getting away and watching the drama unfold. The sight oddly transfixed me. Tabia grabbed my hand and dragged me on. We ran. And then we were outside the campground and we stopped. And here we stayed. There's nowhere else for us to go. Nothing for us to do. Except wait for God to introduce our unknown future to us.

32

"In the midst of Israel."

"Sekani, can you help me out here, please?"

"In a second. Just let me work out where this rope is supposed to... Oh never mind. I'm coming." Sekani emerges from under the fabric of our half-constructed tent with a grin on his face. He finds everything about our new lifestyle amusing. "How do these people do it? Every time we move, I'm going to spend half a day trying to make this thing stay up!"

"I need you to get me some more water for the washing."

"And that's another trek down to the river! The fun never stops!" I laugh. Sekani isn't really moaning. He's fascinated by the way the Israelites survive while on the move. It's a big change from having food brought in from the fields and water running in springs and having a permanent roof to sleep under.

When the army had returned from Jericho, we waited to see what would happen to us. Eventually, we were taken into the Israelites' camp. We've been given a home here: a few tents to house the family and the basic equipment for cooking meals and washing clothes. We've also been adopted into one of the "tribes". Daya has been explaining to me that there are 12 of them and that everybody belongs to one. It's a bit odd really, but she says it helps everyone know where they belong. Each has their own special place to camp around the tabernacle. I don't know much about that yet, apart from that I'm not allowed to go inside. Actually, I haven't dared go near it at all, just in case.

For the first few days, I was scared to talk to anybody and hardly came out of the tent. I didn't want to risk being seen. I was worried how people might react to having Canaanites living in their camp, particularly as they'd just slaughtered a whole city of them. I hid in my bed and only crept out for food and water when everything was quiet. Eventually though, after hearing Sekani's stories each evening, I got too curious and came out of hiding. I was surprised how friendly and helpful everyone is. Mostly they've heard the story of the red cord and the family that protected the spies and want to know all the details. I'm actually getting a bit bored of talking about it now. But not one person has suggested we shouldn't be here and I haven't had a single hostile look. That's more than I can say for life in Jericho, so it's a pleasant change, even though there's more work for us to do and not much free time.

Whenever there is free time, we meet Daya and Gurion. To begin with, we swapped stories of Jericho's final day. I was interested to hear what had happened to them after we left Daya being chased by guards and about Gurion's experience as an army man. They wanted to know our story too. I didn't mind talking about it to them. They had been part of the whole adventure and saved our lives. They deserved to know the ending. Now, we talk about other things. We are all becoming good friends and I'd trust them with my deepest secrets. Sometimes we don't talk. We explore the campground or the surrounding landscape. Sekani is teaching them how to play tricks on people without getting caught. They're telling us all the stories about their God.

It's not all fun and games though. Soon after we arrived there was a big scandal because somebody had kept some of the silver and a bar of gold from Jericho. The tribe of Judah had to go family by family to Joshua until God told him which one was responsible. A man called Achan admitted his crime but because he'd sinned against God, he and his family were stoned and burned. It was harsh punishment but nothing worse than I've seen in Jericho.

Soon we are moving on to Ai. I'm dreading it. I still have nightmares and wake up with vivid images of men with swords and raging fires and collapsing walls. I wake up sweating or shivering before I realise I'm safe. When I do, I thank God that he sent Daya and Gurion to show us our horrible mistake and for giving us a way back in.

Sekani's on his way back with the water. I creep into the tent and hide one of the ropes. I collect the clothes and blankets for washing and wonder how long it will take him to realise. It's a silly trick, but it'll make him laugh.

So, you've finished the book!

Where would you like to go next?

Follow the arrows and then check out the back page to find all the details.

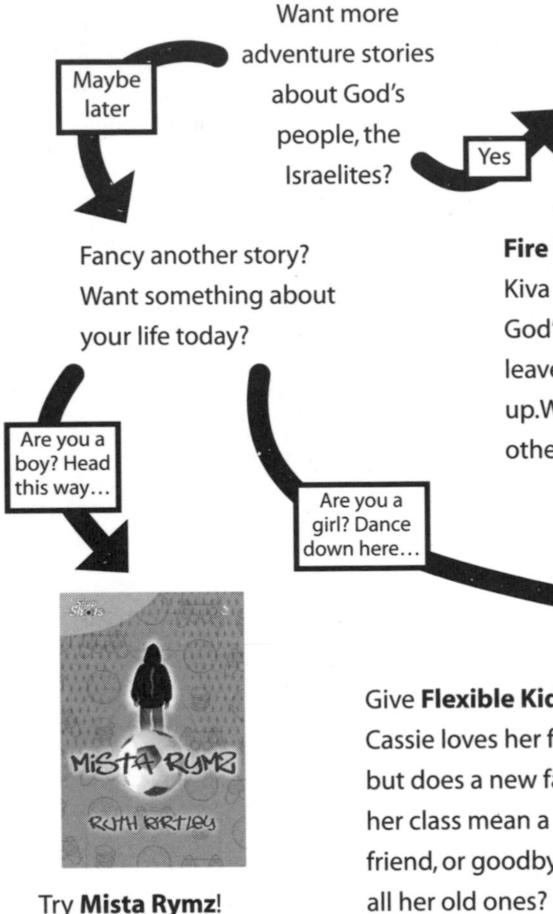

Want more adventure stories about God's people, the Israelites?

Yes

Maybe later

Fire By Night
Kiva and Adalia are two of God's people preparing to leave Egypt, but they get split up. Will they ever see each other again?

Fancy another story? Want something about your life today?

Are you a boy? Head this way…

Are you a girl? Dance down here…

Try **Mista Rymz**!
Wes has got trouble: his cousin Jake. And he has to share his room with him. What could be worse?

Give **Flexible Kid** a try! Cassie loves her friends, but does a new face in her class mean a new friend, or goodbye to all her old ones?

Something else? Want to escape to a different world?

Open **The Book of Secrets**!
Jamie and Rob live in Scotland, but it's not like you know it. The sea has taken over and when they find a book in a seal-skin bag, their adventures start... to threaten their lives!

Dare you wander down **The Dangerous Road**? Gwilym is on his first trip as a shepherd through the dangerous roads of Wales, but he doesn't realise how dangerous this first trip will be.

Find out exactly **Where Dolphins Race with Rainbows**! Luke and Rosie sail into a storm, but when they come out the other side, they're in a different country. A country where battles, revolutions and capture awaits!

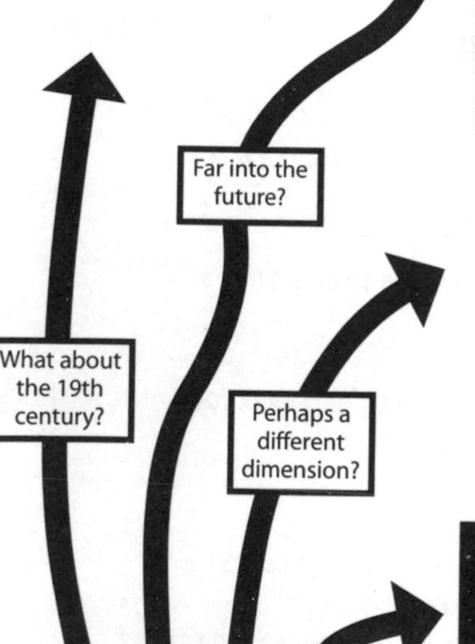

What's it like to be **A Captive in Rome**? Bryn is a Briton, but when his tribe is defeated by the Romans, he is taken prisoner and sold as a slave in Rome!